LOCKDOWN NUMBER ONE

A COLLECTION OF TWENTY
WINNING SHORT STORIES

Edited by Lindsay Fairgrieve

LOCKDOWN NUMBER ONE

A COLLECTION OF TWENTY
WINNING SHORT STORIES

Edited by Lindsay Fairgrieve

ISBN 9798673025987

Published by AudioArcadia.com 2020

Publisher's Note: This book contains adult language and scenes which some readers may find upsetting. The spelling is in English and American, depending upon where the author lives.

CONTENTS

4

*TEN WINNING "GENERAL" THEMED
SHORT STORIES*

*ADDITIONAL   SHORT   STORIES
INCORPORATING "LOCKDOWN # 1" AND
"GENERAL" THEMES*

EDITOR'S NOTE

Never in living memory has the world experienced a pandemic like the catastrophic Covid-19 virus in 2020. It is with this unprecedented situation in mind that we at AudioArcadia.com were prompted to hold our first short story writing competition on this particular subject, in addition to our usual "General" and "Science Fiction" themes.

The twenty winning authors in this anthology live in various parts of the globe – Australia, Malta, Spain, the UK and the USA (hence the variations in spelling). Their biographies, and particularly their experiences during "Lockdown # 1" (and Lockdown # 2 in one particular instance), are diverse and make for captivating reading.

Some of the winning authors have also submitted additional short stories. These form the third section of this book and embrace both "Lockdown # 1" and "General" themes.

AudioArcadia.com holds writing competitions throughout the year. Full details of how to enter can be found by clicking on the "Competition" tab on our website at www.audioarcadia.com

Lindsay Fairgrieve
AudioArcadia.com
September 2020

TEN WINNING "LOCKDOWN # 1" SHORT STORIES

OLIVIA ADAMS lives in Wiltshire and has a background in television, public relations and teaching.

In January 2020 she published "My Elderly Parents – Tales from the Countryside" about the problems of old age and dementia.

In her spare time, Olivia enjoys tending her garden, reading and walking and seeking the perfect flat white coffee.

EXPERIENCES DURING LOCKDOWN

'Lying in bed in the early hours, aware of the silence of the dual carriageway outside my house. A curious quietness that lasts for most of the day. Just broken by the noise of police and ambulance sirens.

One outing a day. A walk across the Downs exploring bridleways and paths around the edges of the barley fields. The sun shines without fail.

Cutting up old clothes to make face masks. One hundred percent cotton, they say, is best. But I was never good at sewing. The needlework nun at school had me tidying the cupboards while my friends made dresses. So my face masks turn out lopsided.

Keeping calm. I'll put the kettle on again. There's not much else to do. I really should be sorting out the folder of old recipes, the boxes of family photographs and the shelves of books I rarely read. Or I could give the house a thorough clean, defrost the fridge, even paint the windowsills. A cup of tea first though.

Do I wear a face mask in the office? Do I step off the pavement when someone is walking towards me? Or drive out to visit my elderly parents in the next county? How much milk and bread do I buy if I'm only going to the supermarket once a week?

"**O**h, I'm not worried if I get the virus," say friends during our online chats. "I'm not in a high risk group. The media is making too much of this." But their faces tell a different story.

Wildflowers. This is my new pastime. Identifying them on my walks. "Herb Robert" and "Jack by the Hedge" greet me as I pass by.

Neighbours. Some I've never spoken to before. We're on the pavement together, clapping and smiling.
   A feeling of solidarity.'

THE COTTAGE
Olivia Adams

Early Saturday morning and through the grimy windows I can see Anna and Dave at the round table. Soup bowls and chunks of crusty bread. Anna turns and waves her spoon when I knock on the window, and nudges Dave's arm. He is very deaf and can't hear my tapping. I beckon to him to open the window and he slowly gets to his feet. He seems pleased to see me.

"Aven't 'ad too many visitors lately,' he shouts, "ad phone calls from yer brothers though.'

'I've left some shopping in the porch, Dave,' I tell him, 'and some flapjacks I made yesterday.'

He nods. 'Birds'll need some corn. It's in the bin.'

I turn to see Dave's robin and several sparrows looking attentive on the bank outside the cottage. Beyond them, in the field of tall grasses, Mr Pheasant is pacing. Waiting. The smell of honeysuckle wafts in the air.

'How are you, deary?' calls my mother.

I notice how frail and disengaged she is. Always polite. But not really sure who I am.

I tell her I'm fine. That I'm still working at the hospital. The department is not too busy. The weather is beautiful, so at the weekends I take long walks across the downs.

'Would you like a cup of tea, deary?'

I explain that I can't come into the cottage

because of the virus.

'What is a virus, deary?'

She has asked me this before. Many times.

'Finish yer soup, Anna,' says Dave. 'Don't want it to get cold.'

He turns back to the open window. 'You don't need to bring shopping,' he tells me. 'I can get it down the town.'

'But Dave ... '

I am exasperated.

'Please don't go to the town, Dave. Stay home. We can order shopping online for you. Or the village shop will deliver to the cottage. And the neighbours are bringing you cakes and bread and milk ... '

I pause. Dave has a look which tells me that he is not listening.

'You don't have to go shopping, do you? You can FaceTime us and tell us what you want ... '

'I don't know what I want 'till I see it, do I?' he declares stubbornly. 'Now, can you feed them birds for me. I wear a mask when I go down the town,' he adds.

Tall grandson had to replace a fuse in the cottage two weeks ago when the electricity failed. He gave Dave and Anna a mask each to wear. This is the same mask Dave is wearing to the supermarket and the chemist and the village shop. Day after day.

'I put it safe in me pocket next to me handkerchief,' he tells me, 'and put it on when I go in a shop.'

Right.

He limps into the garden. I move to the stone seat by the front door so that he can sit on the log box by the window. Then he has a view across the fields.

'You want a coffee?' he asks me, then corrects himself. 'Course you can't.'

He rolls up his shirtsleeves. The sun is hot.

'Bin wearin' me vest this week as it's so hot.'

I smile. I've been offering to buy Dave some T-shirts for months, but he always refuses.

'Ain't no cases round 'ere anyway.'

'How do you know that, Dave?'

'I'd know,' he insists, grinning.

I can see the gaps in his teeth. Sometimes he doesn't bother with the dentist. Just pulls them out himself.

'If people are ill, they have to stay at home,' I say, 'so you wouldn't see them in the town.'

'Word would get about though,' he claims, banging down his coffee mug on the log box. 'It's all up north of the country.'

I feel helpless. The websites show that this area is one of the worst affected.

The front door is opening slowly. Anna clings to the handle as she peers around it. Her long skirt trails across the doormat.

'Would you like to come in, deary?'

'She can't come in, can she, 'cos of the virus!'

shouts Dave.

'Oh no, deary.' Anna is puzzled. She shuts the door.

'Driving me mad she is,' exclaims Dave. 'The other mornin' I emptied 'er hot water bottle and she'd filled it with bloody tea ... tea! And then I went to me teabags and she'd put one of them powder puff things in there. All powder in me teabags! I didn't know what to do.'

My poor stepfather. Nearly ninety years old and trying to look after someone with dementia.

'The carers are coming in to give Anna a bath, aren't they?' I ask him.

Dave's attention has wandered to the bank where Mr Pheasant and several females are feasting on the corn I have thrown them.

'Oh, yes. Them carers coming in are me sunny uplands.'

We laugh.

We are surrounded by pots of bright flowers, lovingly planted by Dave. Pansies, rhododendron, verbena. And up on the bank is aquilegia and London Pride. I think they are Anna's favourites. Purples, mauves and pinks. She has always worn lovely clothes in those colours.

Dave talks me through their purchase and planting and watering requirements.

He puts down the watering can and moves closer to me. I move further along the stone seat.

Instinctively.

'Had a call from the McEnerys. You remember them, don't you?'

'The McEnerys? No, Dave. I never met them.'

'Friends of yer brother's. Their son Paul. They rang me and wanted Sam's number in Australia. Paul died recently. In the chemist shop.'

'Oh my goodness. What happened?'

"E just collapsed and died. In the chemist shop. Lived in New York, I think they said.'

He lumbers into the house to refill his coffee mug. I fetch my mobile from the car and scroll through Facebook. My brother has posted his distress at his friend's sudden death in a drugstore. He was fifty-one. It was Covid-19.

'Dave, I'm afraid it was the Coronavirus. The McEnery's son was ill with the virus.'

Dave is momentarily shocked. 'They didn't tell me that. I don't reckon that's right. They said it was his heart. 'E 'ad a heart attack in the chemist. Heart attack. That's what it was.'

We are silent for a while. Dave peers into his coffee mug and scratches his arm where the eczema is annoying him.

Anna has heard us talking and comes to the front door again.

'Would you like a cup of tea, deary?'

'Thank you, but I've just had one, Anna,' I lie.

'I'd shake it off,' says Dave, returning to the virus. He is clearly concerned.

'An' if I die, I want one of them no-fuss funerals. Straight to the crematorium. You know the ones I mean.'

He turns to see my reaction. His eyes are exceptionally blue against the sky.

'Well, yes, Dave,' I agree. 'I think large gatherings are not allowed at the moment anyway. But if they were ... well, funerals are for the living, aren't they? To help the living grieve for the person who's died.'

'Yer not spending money on no funeral for me.'

He has said this before. Dave has spent his life in the countryside. He has a practical view of life and death. Old people should be as independent as they can. When your parents get old and infirm, they come and live with you until they pass on. Buried in the churchyard beyond the manor.

We are quiet for a while. Anna holds on to one of the posts that supports the porch. Swaying slightly, her spine is disfigured by osteoporosis.

'Where's yer shoes, fatty?' shouts Dave.

Anna is used to this. She looks down at her socks and then away across the fields. 'I don't need them at the moment, Dave.'

He shakes his head and mutters something. His white hair is like cottonseed in the breeze.

'Can we go home now please, Dave?'

'Are you all right, Anna?' I ask her.

She stares at me for a moment. Uncertain of who I am.

'I've got so many aches and pains, deary.'

'Where are they, Anna?'

'Oh, I don't know, deary. Lined up in suitcases for me, I think.'

Dave gazes at her blankly. They have been together for over fifty years. But it is an odd match.

'So, can we go home now, Dave?'

'We ARE bloody home!' shouts Dave. 'Where's this home you want to go to?'

'Up the lane somewhere,' Anna replies, frostily.

There's silence in the garden. Just the squabbling rooks across the field.

'Come on in and I'll make you some tea.' Dave struggles to his feet and offers her his arm to lean on.

'I must head off,' I tell them, blowing kisses across the hot still garden.

'See you next Saturday then,' shouts Dave.

I've left the car at the bottom of the lane. Out of the way. If I park outside the house, Dave will try to 'see you out', as he calls it. Whilst wobbling on his elderly legs. I'm always worried I will run him over.

The roads are almost abandoned. The occasional resident crossing, with a small dog on a lead.

Home, I say to myself as I drive away through the quiet village. The only safe place.

JANE CRITTENDEN, who lives in Hove, East Sussex, is a freelance homes and interiors journalist and is always on the hunt for lovely house projects to write about. She has been creating stories since she was a child and "Escape" is her first published short story.

Jane has a passion for travel and holidays and set her first novel in Auckland, inspired after a three-year stint living there. She's currently working on her second novel, partly set in Barcelona, and a collection of short stories based in New Zealand.

EXPERIENCES DURING LOCKDOWN

Jane writes in her garden cabin and in cafés, usually when her two children are at school. Lockdown instantly stopped the juggle in the daily routine – no school runs or kids' clubs, less work – and introduced home-schooling, regular family mealtimes and evening beach walks.

Jane experienced more time in her day, which became the platform she needed to finish her novel and prepare for publication. In the "new norm", she's much happier with the harmonious balance between family life, work and story writing.

ESCAPE
Jane Crittenden

He looked as though he might cry and he said he'd kill himself.

Alison had heard many things come out of her husband's mouth but this one was new. She thinks about her washed and ironed clothes, folded and ready.

Then yesterday when the news screamed across their TV, their phones, tablets and laptops announcing, STAY HOME!, Alison knew she'd left it too late. Now she's pressed up next to him on the grey velvet sofa he chose, watching his TV. She picks at the white fluff moulting off the cushions. The sofa fabric has a sheen that attracts the stuff.

'Isn't this nice?' he says. He's got his arm around her. It feels heavy on her shoulders. 'When was the last time we sat and watched TV? Let alone on a Monday morning.' His laugh sounds victorious. 'No more books to mark. Time the parents put the effort in.' He tugs her closer. 'I've got you to myself,' he whispers. 'Look at all the free time we'll have together.'

Alison wants to stretch out her crushed shoulder. She hopes her Pilates class goes online. She sees the lovely expanse of evenings alone slip away as the diary is no longer needed. Previously, her husband liked to FaceTime her from hotels in Hawaii, New York, Florida – wherever his route took him. He'd position himself on a lounger by the pool, or sit on a stool at the bar, always with a mocktail in his hand, decorated with a jolly paper umbrella and a slice of fruit hooked over the rim.

She knew what he would say: 'Cheers, sweetheart!' Raise the cocktail glass. Alison would always wave back. 'Don't worry, no alcohol, got to fly the plane soon. I've got a big responsibility, too many lives at stake. No drinking and flying allowed here!' Hearty laugh. Slurp. 'Hope you're being good at home! Not inviting any strange men back while I'm gone!' Another hearty laugh. Gulp, gulp. 'Where are you?' Face comes close to the camera. 'At work still?' Sigh, slurp. 'You really should give up that job.' Or: 'Sweetheart, are you lying on our bed? Teasing me?'

Alison knew he'd recognise the bed sheets. He liked his bed. He preferred to be at home. No duvet, but proper crisp white bed linen with hospital corners, folded and tucked.

Mouth goes back to slurping. 'Better go, sweetheart, I need my beauty sleep. Got a plane full of folk to fly tomorrow. They're relying on me to get them home safely. Big responsibility! Bye.' Blow kiss. Alison would always blow a kiss and wait for the screen to go blank. Then she would end the call. Alison will miss him FaceTiming her. She can't end the call here.

The man on the TV snarls and pushes his girlfriend to the floor. Her blonde hair flops sloppily over her face.

'I won't have any free time, I'm still working,' she says.

There's no school, not in the normal sense, but it's the Easter holidays soon. She thinks of Barcelona.

'Not properly. You'll have loads of time to catch up on housework and stuff. This place is a tip.'

Alison looks around the room. The weekend newspapers are already folded away in the recycling bin outside and she's vacuumed the carpet, the rug and the white fluff off the sofa. Another set of identical white cushions are plumped and straightened against the backs of the matching grey chairs opposite them.

A new diffuser sits on the mantelpiece: sandalwood. Its spicy scent clogs her nose, but her husband doesn't like citrus scents (too acidic) or flowery scents (too girly) and so sandalwood it is. Powerful and masculine.

'I've got to teach online,' she says. 'The kids need support. They can't be expected to do the work I set without any help.'

'*I* need support! It's time for the parents to step in. They'll be at home with nothing to do. Let them carry the burden for once.' He pinches the skin on her shoulder and she winces. 'I keep telling you to quit the job. It's not as if we want the money. It's peanuts. You may as well become one of my special hosties. You'd earn more serving drinks and food on my plane than teaching.' He smirks. 'And their uniform is *very* sexy.'

Alison thinks about the polished women circling the pool and the bar. She thinks about the uniform he brought home when they first met; hanging in the wardrobe. She thinks about the tuition classes she runs when he's away. Cash only.

'Bet you're glad we didn't have any kids!' He squeezes her sore shoulder; consoling as if it was a struggle rather than a choice. 'Little shits suck up all your time at school. Can you imagine being in Lockdown with our own as well?' His laugh is triumphant.

Alison stares out of the window. It's ten in the morning and a beautiful, bright sunny day. The cornflower blue sky reminds her of Barcelona. It's the kind of day that should be full of promise.

Spring is coming; except it isn't. Not inside these four walls. The laughing gods are looking down on the world and saying, *Yep, humans, you tried to kill Planet Earth and now Planet Earth is trying to kill you! But if you sit tight and do as you're told, it will pass – and, in the meantime, here's some sun to keep your spirits up!*

Perhaps she'll have to turn to religion. Become a Catholic; purify her thoughts. But that would mean confession.

A shriek from the TV jolts Alison. The blonde woman is still on the floor, screaming and crying as the man shouts over her. Alison wants to tell her to *Get up! Shout back! Punch him in the face!* Then:

Actually, no, don't, there's never violence. She gazes out of the window again.

Outside. Who'd have thought "Outside" would become the threat. A place they were no longer allowed to go. She wriggles out from under her husband's arm and stands up. She goes over to the window. Both their cars are parked on the gravel drive and the wooden gate is shut. They've imprisoned themselves in their home – as they've been told to. The fortress of leylandii along the front fence is helping the cause, their leafy green branches spreading wider and taller each day. Her husband planted them last year. Alison can only see the tops of the houses across the street.

Something catches her eye. There's a little face pressed against the window of an attic room. She waves. The child waves back. Her heart constricts and she looks up and away, back at the blue, blue sky.

She wonders what Barcelona is like this morning. She shuts her eyes and imagines wandering through the ribbon of lanes off Las Ramblas. Sometimes she would round a corner and walk into a pretty square, surrounded by beautiful old buildings and she'd tip her face to that blue, blue sky, letting the sun warm her cheeks. Waiters bustling between tables of smiles, chatter and laughter, enjoying espressos and ice-cream. Now the shutters will be down, the chairs stacked and it will be silent.

Barcelona isn't meant to be silent.

Alison throws open the window and sucks in a lungful of air. Air! She wishes it was sea air. Like the salty morning breeze that slips through her open bedroom window in Barcelona. Her sheets are crisp and white – with folded hospital corners.

'Shut the window, Ally, it's freezing!'

Alison turns around. The blonde woman has stopped screaming. The man's helping her up. He kisses her tears away and cups her face. He'll glance over at her with tenderness in a minute and the woman will smile and melt into his arms and they will kiss.

Alison looks at her husband. He's watching the TV blankly, sprawled out across the length of the grey velvet sofa, feet resting on the white cushions. He won't appreciate the white fluff on his socks.

'We'll be all right, won't we?' It seems as if he might cry.

Alison thinks about her washed and ironed clothes, folded and ready.

She doesn't know.

❁ ❁ ❁

LAURA DANIEL is a high school English teacher with novelist ambitions, living in rural Missouri. If it worked for Stephen King, maybe it will work for her? Her preferred genre to write in is young adult science fiction or post-apocalyptic scenarios. Her favorite things to do include writing, reading, cooking, and running.

Most of Laura's best writing ideas come to her when she's out running on gravel roads in the middle of nowhere.

EXPERIENCES DURING LOCKDOWN

Laura has been pretty much holed up in her house since Friday, March 13th, which was the last day of school.

She is self-quarantining with her two children and trying to stay sane while adding virtual and home-schooling to the mix. Four months of isolation has made her understand the protagonist of the following short story a little better. When she finds the time, she has been diligently working on her latest novel, a young adult Christian/science fiction combination about a post-Rapture world.

END OF THE QUARANTINE
Laura Daniel

He scratched the final tally mark into the crumbling brick basement wall with an old black grease pen he'd found on her late husband's workbench. Fourteen days had come and gone. He counted them by the dim light filtering through the opaque, block glass window. He didn't know if the days were sunny or cloudy or cold or warm. All he knew was that enough time had gone by.

He was no longer contagious – never had been – and she had to let him out.

Shuffling across the basement floor, he made his way to the rickety wooden staircase. His bare feet crunched on loose bits of cement, some sticking to his skin with the damp. With his arthritic knees, it was a chore to pull himself up those stairs, daily. Especially after sitting and sleeping on the cold cement floor this long. Yet he did it every day to beg her for mercy. She always said no; he had to wait fourteen days to be sure. Then she would leave behind a cold can of chili at the top of the stairs when she was sure he'd gone back down. He piled the cans in the corner – the growing pile was as good an indication of the passing of time as the grease pen tallies – and they were starting to smell.

He raised a fist and knocked on the door.

No answer.

He knocked again. Then, he heard her footsteps

across the floor. As familiar to him as his own mother's, or his ex-wife's. He had lived with this woman for nearly a decade and, although she wasn't his wife, he felt he knew her as well as one. Her containment of him had not surprised him and he didn't hold it against her.

He only knew he needed out or they didn't stand a chance.

He heard her labored breathing on the other side of the door. Years of cigarette smoking had settled in and given her COPD, though she denied that was the cause. The slightest bit of physical activity had her breathing as if she'd sprinted around the block. He usually did most things for her; how had she been getting along these past few weeks?

'Mary?' he called. 'You've gotta let me out of here. The pigeons need tending to.'

She sniffed and then tried to speak, her voice taking on the high-pitched quality it got when she cried from grief or terror. He had heard that tone more and more as the years went by.

'I– I– went out to try to do it myself. But I couldn't, Matt. It's so bright out there.'

'I know, I know. I can do it. It's been fourteen days. Please let me out.'

The doorknob jiggled but did not turn the whole way. She was breathing heavily on the other side, the sound of crying mixed in.

'You can do it. It's going to be fine. I didn't get it. I haven't even sneezed down here.'

'I know. But I'm scared. So many people have died. And how am I surviving?'

'You're surviving because you're smart and you didn't let yourself get infected.'

She was placated by this, because the doorknob jiggled again and then turned. He went down by two steps to let it swing open. She was there, her silhouette framed in the doorway with light surrounding her.

'Oh, Matt.' What had been sniffles turned to full-on tears. She held out her arms to him and he climbed the last two stairs. They stood there, hugging. She felt thinner. They'd been on a steady diet of canned vegetables for the past few months and it had whittled away at both of them, despite the lack of activity.

He held her for a few minutes. It was strange for him, even after all these years. She'd once been married to his good friend. She made no secret of the fact that she wished he had lived. And yet, they had a good thing going as well. But sometimes he worried it was better for him than for her.

So he would do what he could to take care of her.

He looked down at the top of her gray head – the blonde hair dye had long run out – and pulled away. 'I've got to check on them.'

'Okay. I'll make you instant coffee while you're gone. And breakfast. Anything you like. The gas stove is working today.'

'I don't think we've got anything I want to eat.'

He thought about the canned chili she'd been leaving at the top of the stairs for him.

'I've been saving some things back. I can make you fried bread. And pigeon eggs, if they laid any.'

'They don't lay when they're stressed.'

A look of guilt crossed her face. 'You better get out there.'

He grabbed his coat from the hook, not bothering with fixing himself up, even though he could smell the unwashed scent of his hair and clothes. The pigeons needed him.

It was a wind-still day outside. Hot for spring. The pigeons were eerily quiet until he got close. Then they began clucking. They were distressed. Bird shit and feathers everywhere. Three of them were dead. He wanted to save them to eat but he wasn't sure how long they'd been dead and if it would be safe. Instead, he buried them behind the coop in shallow graves.

'Sorry, guys,' he apologized. He wiped away a tear. He loved his pigeons.

After that, it took him the better part of two hours to clean out the coop. There were a couple of eggs, but they were old. Hopefully they'd start laying again now that he would be caring for them regularly.

'It's gonna be okay, guys.' The comforting more for himself than the birds.

The fried bread was cold when he returned but he

dipped it in honey; it was fresh enough and he told her thanks.

'If only the microwave worked.' Mary sighed from her perch at the end of the bar where she sat most of the day, every day.

'Can't imagine the power is going to come on any time soon,' Matt speculated. 'You know, when I fought in Vietnam, we were without power for days. We drank from the creek and there were huge alligators in it. One almost bit my face off. In fact, I've got a little scar.' He pointed to his beard which hid the scar.

'Oh, Matt. Your stories.' She rolled her eyes, then a coughing fit overtook her and she grabbed for her inhaler.

What would happen when the inhalers ran out?

As far as they knew, the world had ended. Family had stopped calling in to check on them a couple of months ago. The neighbor who used to leave fresh produce at the end of their driveway ceased that practice weeks ago.

When Matt went out fourteen days ago to look for food, there were no clerks in the store. Most everything was picked over. But he managed to find some canned food and left a few dollars on an empty checkout lane. He figured it was the little, honest gestures which kept society moving.

While he was out, he hadn't been brave enough to knock on any doors.

But since returning to their isolated country

house, he'd been mad at himself for being such a coward. He should have looked for survivors while he was out there. He and Mary couldn't be the last two people on earth; if they were alive, there had to be more. The pigeons could help. He could send them out as messengers. But they needed to recover first.

He would have to talk her into it. She wasn't keen on the idea of anyone coming here.

He went to the bathroom and took a long, cold shower, thankful they had a well and could get clean, thinking about a plan of action. Planning helped him keep his mind off reality. The reality that he and his common-law wife might be the new Adam and Eve, but with no hope of propagating the species.

He came downstairs to find Mary writing furiously in a notebook.

'What are you doing?' he asked.

'Writing down my stories.'

'Why?'

'I don't have anybody to talk to any more. And if someone comes along after we're gone, they'll know who we were.'

'I wasn't aware that you liked to write.'

'I don't,' she frowned. 'I'm getting this callus on my middle finger.' She held up her hand and showed him.

'Jeez, didn't mean to piss you off,' he joked.

'I'm not flipping you off,' she laughed. 'I used to

get this callus in school when I took notes. I thought it was gone for good, but writing for one afternoon and it's back.'

'You're just like Blake,' he pointed out.

With the mention of her probably-dead, bestselling author son, her eyes filled with tears again. She shook her head and bent to her work, writing. Matt walked past, stealing a glance at the notebook. He saw her husband's name, Wade, in amongst the words. It made him sad.

'I'm going to send the pigeons out,' he proclaimed, heading for the instant coffee.

'What good is that?' Her voice was clipped, pissed.

He expected as much.

'I'll tell people where we are,' he admitted.

'I don't want people coming here.'

'If they've survived until now, they're not going to give us anything. They're not sick.'

'I can't take that chance. I'll die.'

'Being stuck here is as good as being dead.' Even as the words came out, he knew he shouldn't say them.

'You think you'd rather be dead than here with me?'

'You're the one sitting there writing about Wade.'

She glared at him, eyes watery.

Then the crunch of gravel sounded on the driveway. They peered out of the dining room window. Sure enough, a four-door, black, nondescript sedan came up the drive.

'Who could it be?' he asked, grateful their argument had been interrupted. With any luck, this would provide enough distraction that he might be forgiven by default.

She could really hold a grudge, though. He shuddered, remembering being locked in the basement. It was as much about her being angry with him for leaving to find supplies as it was worry about him being contagious. He hadn't seen anybody. He told her that. There was no way the virus was out there on surfaces or in the air. It was spread by people.

And until the car came up the driveway, he'd thought they were all gone.

'Get the gun, Matt,' she commanded.

'It could be anyone,' he protested. 'They could be here with good news.'

'They could be infected.'

'Or perfectly healthy.'

'If I get the infection, I die. You gonna bury me in the yard, by your pigeons?' she demanded, her voice dripping with hostility.

He shook his head slowly, then went to the door and grabbed the shotgun. One bullet. Enough. There was only one person in the car.

'I'm going to talk to him first,' Matt replied.

'Shoot first,' she commanded. 'We talked about this already.'

They hadn't talked about it; she'd told him the

only people to be out were probably people looking for food. And people do desperate things for food. Or to take over a house like this in the middle of nowhere with a good view of everything coming from any direction. He hadn't agreed – not everyone was only out for themselves – but he didn't want to argue then.

Or now.

He nodded grimly and went outside to the porch, holding the shotgun at the ready.

If he recognized the person, he wouldn't shoot. He couldn't.

An unknown man got out of the car. He was wearing a suit. There was a gun holstered to his waist. He reached for it when he saw Matt.

'Sir, I'm putting my hand on my gun but only because I see you have one. If you'll put yours down, I will, too.'

'Can't do that. You first. I've got a very scared lady in here.'

'I'm afraid I'm not able to do that. Please, lower your weapon.'

Matt's finger sweated on the trigger. He didn't know what to do. Mary would never forgive him if he let this man in.

In a split-second decision, he aimed and pressed the trigger. He'd always been a good shot. He didn't hit the stranger in the head where he aimed, but in the neck.

The man fell. His blood spurted all over the grass.

He reached into his breast pocket, pulled out a piece of paper and threw it away from himself. The edge was already soaked with blood. Then he lifted his gun and aimed it at Matt.

'Wait a minute. Maybe we can get you fixed up. Mary, she was a nurse ... '

The man shot anyway.

The world went black.

Three hours later, slowly, slowly so she didn't lose her breath, Mary emerged from the basement where she had been cowering near Matt's empty chili cans. They stank.

How could she have left him down here after everything he'd done for her? And now he was dead. Had to be.

She couldn't leave dead bodies outside. But then again, how would she ever have the strength to bury them?

But she had to see for herself.

Matt was the first one she came to. Dead on the stairs of the porch, twisted in a strange position. Eyes wide open. But she'd buried one husband and Matt didn't have that title. She could live without him.

She stepped over him and went for the other man. His eyes were closed and he looked peaceful.

A piece of paper lay on the ground next to him. If it had been a windy day, it would have blown away. As it was, she picked it up and read it.

Survivors community. No virus. Des Moines, IA.
Mercy Hospital. Use this as your ticket to get in.

The pigeons clucked in their coop.
She crumpled the note and stared at the sky.

BRIAN JOHN FEEHAN is a writer and theatre director, living in Connecticut. His fiction has appeared in "New Millennium Writings" (Muse Award), "The Foundling Review" and "Plots with Guns". His writing was a finalist for the Beverly Hills Film Festival as well as the Heideman Award at the Actors Theatre of Louisville.

He has attended the Iowa Writers' Workshop, has five published plays – (published and rights managed by Heuer Publishing) – and has just completed his first novel, "MUMFORD".

And the rest? Brian's never tasted coffee (and does not intend to), his mother was in the Miss America pageant, he became ill with elevation sickness while trekking the Himalayas, which he would not recommend (the sickness, not the trekking, which was tremendous). In addition, he's jumped from a plane, on purpose – not by accident – and lives with his husband in a two hundred and fifty year old house with two ghosts and a mortgage.

EXPERIENCES DURING LOCKDOWN

The house in which Brian lives was built in 1765. As he has been looking out its windows while sheltering in place, he has been thinking about what its previous inhabitants witnessed through the centuries. They watched as the British Army marched up his road towards the Battle of Danbury in the American Revolution – and again as the army streamed back in retreat. They sent their husbands, fathers, brothers and sons to the Civil War and waited for some of those who would never return. They sat in masked fear during the last pandemic of 1918. They made it through World Wars I and II as well as the Great Depression. They watched, through pioneered glass, the first civil rights protests, a string of assassinations, veterans returning from the Vietnam War and Watergate. Its occupants discussed Reaganomics, the Aids crisis and the Iraq War; and have, as most of us, debated current politics and policies.

And through it all, the house survived, filled, at times, with love, laughter, and loss. Brian and his husband are a part of that legacy. As they have made their way through their own bit of history, Brian has reconnected with old friends (and old stories), written obsessively, forged ahead discovering new foods, or childhood comforts, read, gardened, languidly worried, and anxiously relaxed while knowing that his presence during this Lockdown will be woven into the story of this house for whatever future inhabitants might populate it. His house has seen its share of history – including this latest pandemic – but history will go on. As so shall we.

ENNUI, ADIEU
Brian John Feehan

Old Quigley was convinced he was becoming a curmudgeon. Everything upset the man and not a thing consoled; the curve on a chrysanthemum or cacophonous complaints from some discordant car triggered irritation and prodded the man towards an apocalyptic deed.

And then came the contagion and the rain.

Young Eldritch was entirely expended by the weather. It had been pouring for seventy-two hours without pause and he felt as if he was living in a fishbowl in reverse. The atmosphere's incessant sibilance wreaked havoc on his fevered brow and he was satisfied that – were the downpour not to dissipate – he would be forced into doing something epically irreparable.

Were the men not to have met or stars align or puzzle pieces fit; were the two to have remained inert, alone, aloof, apart; were the weather to have ceased and sunlight be allowed to shadow, the deed would not have been done.

But they did.

It did not.

And it was.

Little Magdalena had marinated all that she could in the Chapel of Little Hope, where she had submerged herself when the deluge had begun – lighting votives, genuflecting, resurrecting old alliances in anticipation of the end of times; underneath the decorated ceiling, sitting in a pew that was molding to her shape.

Young Eldritch had negotiated every solitary inch of his two-room flat for the past thirty days – he had dusted, drowsed and dabbled all he might. No way could he remain inside for an instant more, for a limit had been reached. Even though forecasters warned of wind and hail and of droplets' downward tines, he heaved on his galoshes, mackintosh and cap and hazarded into the fracas, unsure of what awaited.

Old Quigley evaluated his desire to evacuate. The walls were marching inward, of this he was convinced. He came to the decision not to heed the dire warnings but circumvent the regulations to sequester in safe harbor. Adorning anorak and gaiters, brimmed hat and umbrella, Old Quigley locked his door and negotiated five unwelcomed flights.

Little Magdalena had been warned about the scourge and knew where it was heading, though she was unaware of just what form, unaware of just what shape it took. Magdalena had never met Young Eldritch, and had no knowledge yet of Quigley. Little Magdalena was a loner for as many years as she could count and had often prayed for companionship.

Perhaps she should have entreatied a specified conclusion.

Descending stairwells, bitterness bludgeoning with every landing; the septic scent of ramen, roaches mating, sauerkraut, sour mood, Quigley skiffed down stained linoleum towards the door, then strode into a torrent. It was worse than he imagined, (and his imaginings could shock the damned). The storefronts were shuttered, nothing stirred on any streets.

The isolation was not disturbing. On the contrary, the lack of prying eyes incited him to act. He stumbled onward, senses heightened by the rain, pulled in some directionless direction, looking for a schadenfreudeal deed that he could do.

Young Eldritch's shodden feet dissolved into a pond where pavements once had been. Everything was sodden, sopping, saturated (including his desire). He continued on his quest, concentrating on walking between the raindrops and failing each attempt.

Little Magdalena sang a hymn to Him and fingered beads and whispered psalms, unaware of what or who was heading her direction.

Even prior to events, Old Quigley lost his faith in things – in flags and oaths and sealing-wax, in savages and reckonings – convinced that what was once, was lost, but unaware whom to impugn, merely knowing the fault was not his to own.

Young Eldritch never had beliefs, never fathomed that perhaps he should. Instead, he meandered like rainwater on gravel shallows, eluding impediments which threatened. There were none today (besides the storm and all that ails), not a thing to compromise, except the man himself.

Magdelena had intruded to the Chapel, seeking succor like a sucker, abandoning familia while succumbing to her faith. She had not unleashed the rain, or aided in the ailment's spread; nothing she had done had enabled the debility. But, someone had to shoulder blame for an empire's mighty fall.

Ahead of him, a flash of red, resplendent somehow in the rain, intrigued Old Quigley with its edifice; enthralled enough to draw him near.

Young Eldritch saw another adherent heading for a red church door and found himself in blind pursuit, as pliant as a moon-drawn tide.

Old Quigley saw the Younger, and Young Eldritch spied the other, both arriving on the steps of the long abandoned church. Recognizing kindred spirits, the instant eyes connected, in a tempest that no one had predicted, though prophesies foretold and, through the entrance, they proceeded.

From the Chapel's open door poured potato colored light, illuminating Magdalena and her mantilla. She was unaware what lay ahead. First one man, then another intruded on her silent peace, and with them came the weather – a rage once outside now within.

The woman did not belong there, of this Old Quigley was convinced, and he could not brush away her trespass, nor absolve her of what she might have done. They had discovered their redemption. Magdalena filled the bill.

Beside him, the Young Man expectantly awaited his salvation. They had the right to be here. They were right to have come forth. They were in the right and this righteousness adorned them, shielding them from logic, protecting them from empathy. The weight that had debased Old Quigley instantly lifted from his shoulders, taking flight and soaring to the decorated roof.

Young Eldritch found direction where there had once been none; the tedium, the apathy, unbearable dissatisfaction – all were but evaporating with every droplet on the floor.

Little Magdalena whispered her heavenly petitions, even while accepting her entreaties would all but be ignored.

'The time has come,' Old Quigley said, 'to talk of many things.'

Young Eldritch nodded his assent, while descending on their prey.

And to ennui, they bid adieu, delighting in this new diversion.

NICK GILBERT has been writing pieces for creative writing groups on and off for the last twenty years and has had two of them published in a mobile phone magazine some years ago, despite never having owned a mobile phone – thus his interest in the "creative" aspect of writing.

He is a chemist and engineer, recently retired, who spent fifteen years in a firm which made fireproof insulation boards, ten years working in the water treatment industry, plus thankfully shorter periods in less intellectually taxing jobs, including packing branded company biros into plastic condoms and sticking colour-description labels on tins of paint.

Other formative experiences include five years as chairman of a housing co-operative; he is hoping one day that the nightmares thus generated will fade.

Nick lives in Hampshire, far, far, away from the abovementioned place.

EXPERIENCES DURING LOCKDOWN

April: Contract massive sofa-sores from watching complete works of ITV3 and UKTV.

May: Bathroom washbasin slow draining due to old toothbrush heads, snood off my nose-hair trimmer, coagulated toothpaste and hair. Unfortunately, there is a cosmetic porcelain rampart in front of the

45

U-bend. On examination, this porcelain shroud was put in and then the lino was laid around it so it won't shift. Loosen off bolts holding washbasin to wall. No one to hold washbasin whilst I try to waltz the porcelain out the way. Obviously a two-man job. Put off until unsuspecting relative drops in. Can always pour a pint of caustic soda down it if things get serious.

June: Woman from flat downstairs knocks on door to say water from my flat is leaking into her kitchen. Washing machine okay but the cupboard next to the washer is a soggy cave with a waterlogged packet of cornflakes growing a colourful coat of mould. Masked plumber turns up – God help us – Billy the Kid must be spinning in his grave. Tinkers around and cuts hole in wall which reveals water is coming from flat above. Pass on problem and Billy the Plumber. No way will the butchered plasterboard fit back in the hole, so I buy a picture holder of the appropriate size from the pound shop to cover the hole and select a picture of a waterfall to put in it.

July: And so to masks. I'm not washing one mask and a pair of pants every day. "Wash masks like you do your socks", say the newspapers: so once a month it is then. Maybe I'll wrap them round my mobile; that should disinfect them. Where is that 1960's luminous radioactive wristwatch when you need it? I could hang the mask over the open fire on a toasting fork, I suppose, but it would almost certainly end up containing more carcinogens than a packet of Capstan Full Strength cigarettes. I think I'll just microwave them. Oh well, things can only get better, can't they?

August: Decide to use up some time by having planned maintenance on long-term back problem. Pretty nurse straps vibro-massage pads on calves to prevent DVT. Ask if they are useable anywhere else. Cell Block H nurse says only if I sign up for De Luxe laundry package as well.

Hear suggestion that we may have to self-isolate for two weeks after leaving hospital. Say to Drag-Race-Pillar-Medical nurse, 'Is this a***hole protection in case we get Covid-19, or S.O.P. as it's almost certain you'll have given us Covid-19, ha-ha-ha?' She replies 'Probably' in Eastern European accent, before returning to pushing a tumbril of slopping chamber pots towards the horror of the sluice room. Wonder if I should have asked someone more senior.

Sharing ward with two other patients who have elevated temperatures – allegedly for non-Covid reasons – ear-wigging suggests they are serious but not infectious. Thought these sorts of diseases had been eradicated years ago. Very likely they have, outside certain hospitals.

Isn't it amazing to think that one walks past people in the street every day who have to improvise around routine bodily functions.

Shoved out post-haste and post-op, spine braced with a couple of angle-iron brackets, and loaded up with laxatives to ensure nothing basic has been accidentally wrecked.

Spend the first evening at home trying to manage the alchemical mischief of turning the solid contents of twenty-two feet of intestine into a pliable fluid. Now please wash your hands – and arms, and bum, and legs.

September. Now allowed to lie flat on back and convalesce because of back operation. Nurse changes dressing saying 'of course it's waterproof' in answer to polite enquiry. Dressing has swollen to volume of child-size Li-lo, having absorbed approximately one hundred times its own weight in shower water. Zoom book group is OK. Ponder how Zoom ukulele and Zoom handbell ringing groups are faring. Next week is Zoom wine-tasting group. Freed from the constraints of having to drive, or danger of having bus-pass confiscated for rude/unseemly behaviour/vomiting over luggage compartment, there is now the prospect of legions of sozzled OAPs leaning on neighbours' doorbells so they can bend their ears for hours and tell them they 'f***ing well love 'em'. It's an ill wind that doesn't blow some of us some good.

PLAGUE!
Nick Gilbert

Han was worried about the outbreak of London sniffles that was all over the news. On the TV, commuters were marching through railway stations wearing pollution masks, dust masks, and even leftover World War Two gas masks. The vox pops much beloved of TV stations produced mainly incomprehensible mumblings since hardly anyone would take off their masks.

A few attention-seekers put up text messages on their mobiles and held the screens up to the cameras. Most of these communications seemed to be of the "help", "we're all going to die" or "goodbye, Mum" variety.

One particularly tenacious reporter had found a man to speak comprehensibly, but only because he had cut a hole in his mask so he could have a cigarette.

Han felt distinctly at risk as he was a waiter in the Wun Lung Gon Chinese restaurant where obviously customers could not wear masks, and the management had strictly forbidden them to the staff as being prejudicial to confidence in the business.

Han's fiancée, Li, worked in the kitchens and they had been planning to go home to get married with both their families present. His thoughts were vacillating by the minute between whether they could bag a free flight on a Cathay Pacific mercy trip, or whether Li and he would end up in an unmarked mass grave for wheezing aliens somewhere in the Scottish highlands.

'I've tried Embassy twenty times today about Heathrow flights, phones always go beep-beep-beep,' he said.

'You silly boy,' she replied, 'everyone try. My uncle Twitter me – we go Teeside airport get the one a day flight to Amsterdam. If anyone ask, we only go to get cannabis for granny with cancer and we come back. Then we get plane from Amsterdam to Shanghai instead.'

'Har – clever uncle; we not look English in Amsterdam. What happen if all flight booked by other crafty Chinamen with clever uncle?'

'He say if worst come to worst get Trans-Siberian Express to Vladivostok then walk.'

But as it turned out even that gate had shut. The government had cancelled all the trains that weren't on strike which naturally meant the roads were gridlocked.

On the TV, a reporter was saying, 'A couple were thought to have the bug but were merely grossly dehydrated after arriving here at Clacket Lane Services, having taken thirty-six hours to drive two miles. And I've been told they've run out of tea, soft drinks, and throat pastilles – so no help here. Back to you in the studio, Charlene.'

'Thank you, Dean. Government advice is to drink

plenty of fluids, wrap up warm, and stay indoors. The symptoms of the London sniffles Do4U2 virus to watch out for are runny nose, streaming eyes, and an uncontrollable urge to swear at daytime television. The virus is thought to have crossed the inter-species barrier by someone rubbing noses with a rescue dog of dubious antecedents. And now, over to Alistair who is with the Prime Minister outside the emergency hospital which has just opened for quarantining new cases.'

'This hospital has been built amazingly quickly, Prime Minister. Can you tell us anything about that?' Alistair asked.

'Thank you very much, Alastair. Yes, this hospital was put up in a morning by our good friends Bodgett & Leggatt Construction in an absolutely splendid effort, if I may say so. Don't worry if it looks wobbly – it's a bit windy and it's only the camera moving about. And let me assure you there's absolutely no truth in the rumour that it is clad with the same insulation as some old council blocks of flats so that we can torch it if the outbreak gets out of control.'

'Probably fall down before gets dark,' Han said to Li, as they were watching. 'Even if it doesn't, everybody know NHS is NFG because this after all underpaid, understaffed, overworked budget health service with ten month waiting list for abortion. So might as well post a Will on Facebook.'

'We never get to Shanghai. Not even Amsterdam,

not even Teeside,' Li said sorrowfully.

'I no want to live on Teeside; and I definite don't want to die on Teeside,' said Han. 'I've had e-mail from cousin Fong up north, he say he hear they moor old cruise boats in Clyde River and Morecambe Bay for quarantine, and maybe opening old Butlin's Camp in North Wales with barbed wire and armed guards.'

'Old Butlin's Camp in North Wales in December? Even without barbed wire and mines I'd rather go to abandoned ISIS tent city in Syria two miles from nearest drinking water tap,' said Li. 'Luxury by comparison. Do you think we might get to Folkestone and walk through channel tunnel and get sanctuary at immigrant refugee camp in France?'

'I don't think China want us back anyway,' said Han. 'Still don't trust anyone coming from Britain since Opium Wars.'

Han was getting depressed. He could see the likes of himself and Li being herded into cattle trucks and sent to separate death camps in Snowdonia, the Kielder Forest or, worst of all, care homes with suddenly lots of vacancies.

On the TV, Charlene was saying, 'Amazing scenes at registry offices around the country as people want to get married because they think they might die soon – as happened in World War Two. Fighting broke out at a London registry office where an LGBTQ couple insisted they be given priority because they had a compromised immune system.'

'I once had ride in MGBGT,' observed Han. 'Does that make me honorary sex don't-know too?'

'Can we get married now, Han, because I don't think we get to Shanghai anytime soon, and there probably no Buddhist priests on Trans-Siberian train in case we start sneezing?' Li fluttered her eyelashes.

'They can get married but they should not get closer than one metre to each other, according to the government,' said Charlene on the TV, 'as it is thought that the virus can be passed on this way.'

'Okay. We get married, but no cuddling,' said Han. 'Nobody say though we can't have virtual sex using phone. No kissing and cuddling but on bright side we can do it quite safely, you at home on laptop and me mobile on train; as long as I wear mask; and keep hands above waist, of course. Don't even have to wash hands before or afterwards.'

'Han, I know you keep saying you want to try dirty sex but I think you taking advantage,' said Li.

Up on Mars two green skinned creatures in military uniform were watching the live feeds on BBC and CNN.

'Turn the rockets round: I think we'll invade Pluto this year instead,' one said to the other.

SARAH SCOTFORD-SMITH is a mature student studying for a BA (Hons) in English Literature and Creative Writing at the University of Gloucestershire, England. Previously, she was a cake decorator and confectioner. Recently she set up her own blog on which she posts her own stories. She is both a Prose and Dramatic Writer.

Sarah writes in her kitchen surrounded by three crazy Border Collies who howl every time they hear an ambulance siren. She also has three chickens and one cat. She is married and has two grown-up sons who still live at home. She writes with a background of noise and chaos.

EXPERIENCES DURING LOCKDOWN

When England went into Lockdown in March, Sarah had six weeks left of her second year at University to finish off; lectures and workshops were moved online. The Dramatic Writing module had been taking place at the Everyman Theatre in Cheltenham. The aim was that the students' plays would be performed by professional actors in the Everyman's studio theatre at the end of the semester. The showcase was put on hold, to be performed at a future date.

Life in early Lockdown was busy for Sarah. She was working towards her end of the year university assessments and adapting to online learning. Plus, family life had changed; everyone was pushed together at home. Both her sons were furloughed and the eldest one's girlfriend moved in.

Weekends became boozy family occasions; board and card games were played. The weather was often so good that these were played in the garden after a barbeque. It was great to reconnect with the family unit.

Even though Sarah enjoyed having the family around, once a day she would escape to the bluebell woods for a bit of peace and quiet!

THE QUEUE
Sarah Scotford-Smith

I haven't seen a queue this long, outside the village hall, since the rummage sales of the 1970s. Although the one-metre apart distance probably makes it appear longer than it is. At least the distance has been reduced from two metres. It would have been unacceptable for a line of people, waiting for an alcohol abuse meeting, to snake back to Boozy Ben's off-licence. The last thing these people are looking for is temptation.

There is an urgent demand for this meeting. Online meetings won't suffice any longer; everybody has been drinking far too much, but I wasn't expecting this many to turn up. I hope there are enough chairs.

How am I going to adhere to social distance regulations? Maybe I should have booked the local football stadium instead? It would've been outside, so less of a Coronavirus risk. Too late now.

I'm going to have to ask everyone to go home to use their own toilets if they need to go. I'm certainly not going to don my rubber gloves and deep-clean them in-between use.

Look! There's Angela from Number 9. We've become good friends since Lockdown. She's spotted me. Oh, she's turned away.

'Hello, Angela.' I walk towards her and lean forward, at a safe one-metre distance.

'Hello, Clara,' she says, turning around and feigning surprise.

She fiddles with the handle on her handbag; her overgrown bob quivers under a cage of hair lacquer and I notice excessive streaks of grey amongst the blond.

'So, you haven't managed to get an appointment with your hairdresser yet?' I say.

My hair is coiffured to perfection. My hairdresser continued to cut and colour it in her garden throughout Lockdown – not that I'd admit that to Angela.

'No, not yet. I'm waiting for them to email me back,' she replies, glancing furtively further on down the line. 'There's a bit of a queue, isn't there? I didn't have you down as the sort of person who'd hit the booze hard over Lockdown.' Her mascara caked eyelashes flutter as she surveys me.

'I'm not, dear. I'm the alcohol abuse counsellor.'

I lift the black case in my hand and with my other hand indicate my black trouser suit and cerise blouse. I prefer to be business-like as it gives me an air of authority. I rarely divulge my therapy clientele choice to anyone as counselling is an extremely private affair.

'I didn't know you were … ' Angela's face turns the colour of my blouse; she turns her back to me. Well, how rude. She was always friendly on those Thursday evenings when we were out on our front lawns clapping for the NHS. When that clock struck eight, Angela would clap her hands so enthusiastically, her palms would turn crimson and swell. So much so that she'd struggle to hold her *Clap Thursday* glass of Prosecco.

Angela glances away from the queue. I can tell she's thinking of turning back home. She wouldn't be the first. I know the signs. She's shuffling her feet; next, she'll break into a run. I tap her on the shoulder. She turns around.

'You weren't thinking of leaving were you, dear?' I ask, trying my best to adopt my therapist tone.

'No ... of course not. What gave you that idea?' She shakes her head. Her hair barely moves. Hell, that's some powerful hairspray holding that barnet in place.

I don't believe her. I have her down as a runner. 'Why don't you walk alongside me?' I usher her forward with my hand.

'I'm fine here,' she answers, a little starchily.

She wasn't like this on *Clap for the NHS* Thursdays when she was fuelled by Prosecco. She was extremely chatty and loud then, and always reluctant for the evening to come to an end. Her Dave would stand there, cradling a can of beer, appearing uninterested by the whole commotion as if he'd rather be somewhere else – anywhere else.

I hover a moment. Angela lowers her gaze to her feet. I understand. The stigma of alcoholism is something no one wants to be identified with; just standing in this queue is a positive step forward.

Those *Clap for the NHS* Thursdays were fun. Even I would indulge in a glass of socially distanced white wine while Angela told me all about that week's disastrous work Zoom meetings: colleagues standing up, forgetting they hadn't bothered with trousers that day, or amorous pets getting frisky in the background.

As the *Clap for the NHS* Thursdays went by, Angela moved on from a glass of Prosecco to a bottle and started banging a saucepan at eight. Those evenings had something of the Blitz spirit about them.

As I walk along the queue, my case swings back and forth. My back is rod straight because I'm trying to determine an air of importance. Angela isn't the only one of my neighbours here; there are quite a few. As they realise the counsellor is a friend from their street, they sink into their clothing as if they are tortoises dipping their heads inside their shells.

Right now, I feel as if I am more of a Victorian schoolmistress, spreading fear within her pupils, than a therapist. I espy Sally and Steve from Number 12 and wave at them before they can look away.

'Sally and Steve, I'm so glad you're here,' I say. 'I haven't seen you since the last *Clap for the NHS*. I hope you're well?'

Their curtains are always drawn these days.

I hope they haven't had Covid-19.

'Mm ... we've been busy.' Their lips curve upwards, they twist to gaze at each other; their arms are entwined. Before Lockdown they were never together. They led busy working lives and socialised separately. Then, at the beginning of Lockdown, they bought a hot tub and started drinking *Sex on the Beach* fishbowls in the afternoon while playing Eighties music; what a great party atmosphere! They certainly made the most of being furloughed.

Angela called it 'Steve and Sally's sex pond'. She's jealous because she wanted to spend Lockdown drinking *Sex on the Beach* in a sex pond. But Dave's version of it was a day's fishing down on the canal bank which was when we were allowed to exercise for more than an hour a day.

On the final *Clap Thursday*, I was feeling brazen after my small glass of white, and told him, 'Angela wants to share a fishbowl with you.'

He stared at me, puzzled. 'Yesterday, I caught her a nice trout for her tea. She was happy enough,' he said.

I expect Angela misses the comradeship of those Thursday evenings. If I were Angela, I would. I glance back up the line and half expect to spot her making a run for it. But, no, she's still there, gazing at her feet, wondering if they'll act on their own and march her away from this queue.

My long-term regulars are also waiting for the meeting. They're glancing around, surprised by the amount of people. I wave at Mick. I hope he survived. Shortly before Lockdown, he'd been alcohol free for a whole year. I stare at him questioningly. He gives me the thumbs up. At least there's some hope.

Apart from Mick, there is Chris. He's always falling off the wagon. I've had several Team meetings with him during Lockdown, but to no avail. I have to say, he has one hell of a tan. But I'm not surprised. He took his camper to Bournemouth during that boiling hot weekend and stayed overnight; even though restrictions hadn't been lifted at the time. He's a right beachcomber; said the threat of Coronavirus wasn't going to stop him dipping his feet in the sea and getting rat-arsed on the beach.

Oh, it's the Smith family from Number 11. 'It's great that a family with older children are doing an activity together.' I simper, smiling at the boys. Their arms are crossed, and their lips are drawn into straight lines, making them appear solemn. I suspect they've been dragged here.

'Yes, we've become one of those families who actually enjoy spending time and doing activities together.' Sue Smith laughs and ruffles her eldest son's hair. He's in his early twenties. He glowers and shoves her arm away.

'Nope, that's a lie,' adds Adam Smith, the father. 'We've spent so much time together, we got to the stage when we needed to get pissed in order to cope with being in each other's company.'

'Well, I can help with the alcohol abuse, but I can't help you with relationship counselling!' I chortle heartily.

According to Angela, who lives next door to them, since Lockdown began the Smiths have had lots of alcohol-fuelled family games nights. The wrong Monopoly outcome often ended with a tantrum that would outdo a toddler. The only way Angela said she could cope with the noise coming from next door was to reach for another bottle of Prosecco. I'm sure living with Dave is enough on its own to turn her to drink.

It's a shame for those Smith boys, though, as the youngest has just turned eighteen. All they want to do at that age is to go out boozing with their friends. Instead, he's having to put up with his parents' tantrums when he beats them at Monopoly.

Sue turns away to talk to Lorraine Pierce from Number 17. Poor, poor Lorraine – home-schooling has taken its toll. To begin with, she was the model Lockdown parent. Their house was the first one in the street with rainbows in its windows. But then the teachers' demands got too stressful and she became Boozy Ben's best Pink Gin customer. You can almost spot the well-trodden groove in the pavement from Lorraine's house to the off-licence. You can set the clock to the second she closes her front door and makes her way to the off-licence;

it's when that fitness guru keeps the kids entertained with PE. By dinner time, Lorraine has usually reached the stage of teaching the kids mathematics with empty gin bottles. Her husband, James, leaves her to it. He reckons if home teaching was up to him, they'd be playing skittles with beer cans.

I'm at the front of the line. I glance back, wondering if Angela is still there; she's standing away from the queue and her feet are pointing homewards but she's hanging on in there. I need to get the doors open before she makes a run for it. I turn towards them. Ellen and Jim from Number 15 are first in the queue.

'Fantastic, you're both here,' I say, as I wait for them to shuffle a safe metre away from the doors.

'Didn't know this was what you did,' Jim remarks. 'Bit embarrassing because you'll realise how much we drink.' He sticks his thumbs into the inside of his belt and rocks back and forth on his worn leather shoes.

I offer a small smile. Jim and Ellen spent the first week of Lockdown stockpiling toilet paper, pasta and self-raising flour in their garage. I already know how much they drink. Judging by their overflowing recycling bin, toilet paper, pasta and flour weren't the only things they stockpiled.

Considering the length of this queue, those recycling men certainly have their work cut out in this neighbourhood, carting away the empties.

Ellen made some beautiful sponge cakes in those early weeks of Lockdown with all that flour she stockpiled. She regularly left them on the neighbours' doorsteps as a nice surprise.

I miss the comradeship of those early days, but my waistline doesn't. I wonder how many in the queue are planning to stay for the weight control class that follows my alcohol dependency one? After all, I'm not the only person who looks a little rounder now than before Lockdown. Perhaps, if you attend both, you can get a discount?

A flash of colour catches my eye. Angela's making a dash for it. I knew she would. I consider running and catching her arm, but she needs to be ready and she isn't yet. I will talk to her privately. No one enjoys their downfall to be publicly displayed and alcoholics, as with all of us, can be secretive people.

I open my case and take the village hall key out. I'm careful not to open it too wide. I don't want anyone to notice the bottle of white wine I bought from Boozy Ben's. It wouldn't seem right. Don't judge – the world isn't back to normal yet, is it?

ROBERT SCOTT lives in Edinburgh, Scotland, UK. He has short fiction in "Popshot" Magazine, "East of the Web", "EllipsisZine", "Nymphs Publications" and "Bandit Fiction". He was longlisted for the "Bath Flash Fiction Award" in February 2020 and shortlisted for the "HISSAC" short story competition in 2019.

EXPERIENCES DURING LOCKDOWN

Robert feels he has been very fortunate thus far into the pandemic (as at September 2020).

Edinburgh has been even more beautiful, without the usual traffic, crowds and pollution. He has got to know the city much better, having walked down every street within a five-mile radius of his flat.

Robert has also spent a lot of time looking after the tenement's shared garden, which perhaps explains the creative impulse which led to *Winter is for Sleeping* in this anthology.

Of course, the isolation, sadness and suffering, plus the weirdness of it all, never feels too far away. That has also found its way into the story.

WINTER IS FOR SLEEPING
Robert Scott

Spring was sunshine and showers. Early summer switched to warm and stormy.

Jon concluded that he didn't need the weather forecasters. You always found out soon enough. So, he gave up on them, the old familiar faces. They were the first to go. Next were the TV newsreaders, then the radio ones and, lastly, the newspaper journalists. Life became simpler, less cluttered.

The junk mail was harder to stop.

One morning, after breakfast, Jon collected the mass of paper ads which had piled up at the front door. As he cradled them, a folded sheet of yellow paper escaped. As it landed on the doormat, he saw his name, handwritten in blue ink. He dropped the bundle back on the floor and sat by the shoe rack.

Dear Jon,

Hope you are doing ok, given everything. We wrote this because you are not answering your phone or door anymore – even when your lights are on.

It's the garden, Jon. We don't want to trouble you, but you have to do something about it. We have cut down what's coming over to our side. Have you been out there recently? We realise it has been a difficult time, but something needs to be done. You could at least check that stuff we planted for you in March.

The old offer still holds. If you want us to help with anything, or just come over and have tea (we're allowed that now, if you didn't know).

Love and regards,
Ahmed and Lina

P.S. Ahmed will come round with his strimmer, if you like.

Not dated. Probably, a few days old.

The garden. He would take a look tomorrow.

Mid-morning the next day, as Jon glanced towards the front porch, he remembered his neighbours' note.

The air was musty and stale in the dining room. Not a smell he had ever associated with it. Hitting the light switch, he was faced with one of those rooms where someone of note has lived – everything set out as per their illustrious life.

There were six chairs around the table, plus six placemats, and three more down the middle. A crystal vase sat, dead-centre, empty and useless. It had that funny old-fashioned thing in the neck to separate out the stems. It was ready to go; all it needed was a bunch of flowers.

The artificial light cast gloomy, ghostly shadows. The curtains were closed, as they had been since winter. He might as well check what his neighbours were so worried about. He owed them that.

Touching the softness of the green cords had the familiarity of putting on old slippers. He parted the curtains a foot or so. The light flooded in, setting off a haze of dust swirling above the table.

The door of the French windows needed a shoulder barge to get open. Then more pushing to get out. He nearly slipped on a clump of weeds around the base of the steps. Branches and twigs flicked back at his face and splattered against the glass like pellet shots. Was it so long since he had been out there? A couple of steps got him to terra firma, with a head-on view of the garden.

The sun was halfway up in the east. The warm wet weather had turned the old place into a patch of Brazilian rainforest. A head-high thicket, a swathe of every shade of green, stretched away, hiding any sign of the far end of the garden. He shut his eyes and tried to conjure up how it used to be. But an image wouldn't form.

Then he spotted something that he recognised. A single Siberian iris: tall, slender and elegant, rising above the morass. The stem rose, a green rod firing straight up to the sky. Atop was the pointed head – with a marbled pattern of violet-blue and white. Fine, delicate and strong, as if imbued with an intelligent life. Beautiful and independent.

The garden suddenly seemed even uglier and more chaotic. Too much disordered, out-of-control, life staring back at him.

He turned to go inside. Then he thought of the iris. Could he take it in? It wouldn't survive long. He hated to leave it out there, but he had to.

A week passed before he went out again. He finally remembered how the garden used to be. A dream brought it back.

Four aspirin normally got him through until eight or nine, but a commuter's banging car door made it an earlier morning.

He woke to a pillow that was wet on one side, and with a salty estuary of white lines across the other. Behind his retina hung an image of a summer afternoon in the garden from years ago. Wine, music, laughter.

He got dressed and headed out to see how the jungle down there compared with his dream.

The door still needed a shove to get out. Though chilly in the shade, it was clear and bright above the looming canopy of the elder tree. An orangey glow hung over the treetops to his right.

Recalling the dream, he mapped what lay below the overgrowth. A few shafts of light helped, dropping some clues. The roof of the tool shed he put up in '97, the top of the pole for the washing line, an arm of the wooden bench popping out from amongst ivy. But what about the vegetable patch and the cold frames? Near that flapping plastic sheet maybe. Oh, there's some colour – red

– no, surely not? Closer up, it resembled a market stall after an earthquake. Bumper crops everywhere: lettuces, radishes, spring onions, tomatoes, courgettes, the lot.

For the next three days the lunch menu didn't vary. The radish chopped up, with rocket and cherry tomatoes, tasted of curry. The strawberries couldn't have been improved with ice-cream.

Meals were lazy affairs. He ate whatever was within reach. The camping plate and mug sat at the end of the bench. The camping knife in his pocket. A bucket filled from the hose attached to the outside tap served to wash what he foraged and to wash up, if he wanted to.

Before long he was eating his meals outside and almost everything came from the garden. He didn't need much. Finding food, eating, exploring, pruning back the growth with the shears took up most of the day. The bench became his boat in the sea of green.

It was such hassle getting in and out of the house. It was easier to stay outside – the door was getting worse.

When he went inside at the end of the day, the rooms felt stuffy and sad. Whereas, out the back, time flew by; with the warmth, the insects buzzing around, watching the birds, the clouds, and the sun going down.

The clouds were his new TV shows. The simple

mix of blue and white set off hours of observation. The variety of shapes and movement was miles better than anything on the telly.

One mild evening he got lost in them as he wondered, in particular, how many miles across, high and long an unusual cloud was. What was its volume? He lifted a finger and measured it as it moved across a roof, past a chimney pot. A spaceship-shaped cumulonimbus glided towards the town centre, heading to invade. Another seemed to be hiding something that might pop out of a jaggy blue gap at its centre.

That evening was the first time he stayed out for the whole night. No aspirin, no booze. He just fell asleep, comfortable on the cushions and under the tartan travel rug, watching the clouds fade into the twilight.

The following morning, he woke to the blackbird singing and the sun rising. For a moment he felt twenty years younger. He washed in the bucket, splashed under the hose and went to the loo in the bushes at the bottom of the garden. It was like camping as a scout.

He began to spend the next night out too, but the rain started at three in the morning, which sent him running inside for cover. That led to the construction of a makeshift awning, which worked, but the fun of that first night under the stars never returned.

Over the next few days and weeks, temperatures dropped to autumnal levels. The camping gas stove stretched the foraging longer, but eventually the food started running low, along with the novelty of his life outdoors. He slept inside a couple of times.

One late autumn day he realised he had had enough. It was overcast, and the place was grey and sad. The garden had lost the lush bloom of summer. The bench was covered in half-brown leaves – only the odd flower on the cushion pattern popped through.

His time in the garden had been a blessing while it lasted. The place was tidier – simply through his being there, getting food and tools, and exploring – way better than the first day, anyway. He remembered his neighbours' note. They must have noticed the change from their upstairs rooms.

Would he see them again? Would he see anyone again in his self-imposed exile? There was nothing out there in the real world for him. His relatives and friends would be all right without him. They had their lives to be getting on with. But without her, he couldn't be bothered with anyone or anything.

With Lockdown, it was easier. Only him and her at the end. A funeral for two. A stroke, possibly Covid-related, they said. That was before everyone knew what it meant.

He managed to get a grip on the door handle of

the French windows, but it wouldn't budge. The oil was under the kitchen sink – that was what it needed. He gave up; he could try it later. He sat on the bench. It was getting dark. He was extremely tired. He hadn't been eating enough.

He saw it before he felt anything. One leaf then another did that movement as if the invisible man was flicking them. Then a tap, tap, tap somewhere – the sound of a conductor as the audience hushes. Into the opening movement and away. The symphony didn't really get going. No more than a light drizzle with the odd serious drop. One landed on his hand. A change of breeze direction; he shut his eyes.

She used to spray the indoor plants and squirt his face as he followed her about, annoying her. She would fire and run – then he would chase her round the house, after the sound of her giggles.

Don't see anyone, they said. You might catch something. But he didn't want to see anyone. Stupid garden. Stupid suburbs. Six chairs. Ridiculous. They should have gone back to the city. Lived more.

Winter is a time to sleep. Who said that? A flake landed on his nose. He pictured the shapes of the crystals. They had been to a photography exhibition. Was that before they lived in Russia and went skiing with the hired wooden skis, and kept falling over?

So many pale images: complex, delicate, strong, beautiful – there for a dream of a time and then gone, melted away deep into the memory. He dreamt up more designs until he fell asleep.

WIBKE SEIFERT is of German origin. She is married and has three adult sons. The family has lived in Malta since 1995 and Wibke works in the family business as a financial controller. The company has branches spread across five continents which has given her the opportunity to travel and discover what the various countries had to offer.

Being a lover of the outdoors, Wibke has enjoyed mountain climbing and swimming in different places.

She is also a keen artist and her experiences often find their way into her art. She is as passionate about colours and shapes as she is about words. A novel and a collection of short stories were published in 2010 and 2015 respectively which connect her past in Germany to her present in Malta.

EXPERIENCES DURING LOCKDOWN

'Lockdown questioned the life I knew,' says Wibke. 'It threw it from a speedy race to solid ground, and it stumbled. Social contacts disappeared or were replaced by words shared online or over the phone.

Freedom of movement became one-directional: towards close family or internally. At the same time, it was shadowed by an economical thread that nobody could have expected or imagined. But there was also a chance to pause and take stock.

If Lockdown provided for anything at all, it was time, an incredible amount of time. I had to change gear. Reduce my speed of living. Apart from writing, painting and sculpting became important.

I produced objects of light and colour to make up for the difficult situation. My dogs were pleased to have me staying home 24/7 for weeks and months on end.

But my parents missed me. They are of an age where contact with me becomes essential for their well-being. They still live in Germany, one in the north, one in the west. Before Covid-19, they saw us once or twice a year. It hit them hard, knowing that I couldn't leave Malta. Not even in an emergency.

The island was locked down, Germany was locked down. So, my parents and my family started emailing and WhatsApp-ing each other on a daily basis which, for my eighty-two year old parents, was quite a challenge.

I missed my sons. One is in Germany, one in Malta, one in South Africa, and communication, therefore, became essential!

I was in daily contact, via our WhatsApp group, with my close friends in Malta – eight ladies of four different nationalities. We talked about the weather, the number of new Coronavirus cases in Malta, the number in our home countries; we exchanged recipes and complained about how we missed lipstick, high heels, dancing and any old nonsense, due to Lockdown.

I posted what I was painting; another lady posted what she was cooking and some simply posted family pictures.

After two months we switched to Zoom. This meant we had a reason to do our hair again and apply makeup. We grew closer during that time, despite a few arguments. The longer Lockdown took, the more sensitive and a little bitchy we became. But we were essential to each other. Love, caring, and having someone who listens, becomes more important than ever.'

EMPTY SPACES
Wibke Seifert

Boarding pass and passport are not in their customary place. She searches through her handbag and backpack twice and thinks of running back to security but the lady at the front desk suggests, 'Maybe the computer bag?' A stupid idea because she never places her documents there, but nevertheless there they are.

With sweaty armpits, she enters the lounge. Weizenbier, oriental bulgur salad and a colourful tabloid are all she needs. On the first page, the usual picture of the editor with her long, blond hair falling freshly brushed over one shoulder, black trousers and designer blouse, the list of contents along with her note; not once the C-word.

She glances out of the window. No airplanes are taking off or landing, no bustling of towing vehicles, buses or luggage vans. The shops in the hall had been closed; some fruit stalls were open, their lights were on but no one was queuing. Empty spaces.

She checks her phone. There is a missed call, unknown number. It can't be the ministry. She had saved that number from their first call of over a week ago, when she had been sitting at her regular spot by the beach, eating local prawns with rye bread and drinking a glass of Shiraz, lost in her thoughts from that two-hour walk.

The beach had been empty, as was normal at this time of the year, when the North Sea shows off her roughest side. For kilometres not a soul but herself, pulling her cap closer into her face against the north wind, pondering where all her sadness was coming from. She hadn't found an answer, at least not until the phone rang. It had been lying in front of her on the table, next to that funny address list to be filled in by every patron, full name and home address, just in case.

When the phone rang, she had been wondering where her home actually was, here on this island or on the other, where her husband had been waiting patiently for her for almost three weeks. Patiently, because he had granted her this vacation. But patiently doesn't mean without a grumble. And as the phone rang, it dawned on her with a certain clarity that sadness had been her partner for most of her life. Her mum had fled the Russians, her dad his burning home. The phone rang and rang. Childhood memories kept popping up. Her parents had always loaded their share of hope and fear on to her for as long as she could remember, and she had always willingly accepted it.

She puts the phone back into the handbag, the red one which matches the leather backpack. She had bought both items herself, unlike the many bags she had been given by her husband over the years. She closes the zips, the inner and the outer one; the phone inside is on silent.

She flips through the magazine. It is six days old. From a time when restaurants were open and life was pretty normal. A time when even the island hadn't started to shake off its visitors, as a sea lion does when it shakes water from its fur. Last page and she hadn't come across the C-word once, not in the whole magazine. She closes the tabloid and puts it on the table, next to the empty beer glass.

She is sweating. Is always sweating at German airports, winter or summer. They are way too overheated whilst at the Maltese airport she always freezes. Its air conditioner is as cold as ice and she never travels without a scarf. She also never travels without her power bank though now it is neither in the handbag nor in the backpack or even the computer bag. Far too many bags this time.

She looks up. The lounge is quiet. No swishing sheets of newspaper, no jingling of ice cubes, no hectic typing on keyboards. She stares at her watch for a minute, sixty seconds, no movement anywhere in the room. She gets up, puts on her backpack, her PC bag over one shoulder, handbag over the other and marches off. The lady at the front desk says there is ample time but she merely nods and keeps on going.

In the hall to the gates she finds a packing station with two large shelves against the wall, strong enough to take heavy suitcases, strong enough to take her. Two hours before boarding. To the left an open Starbucks counter. She is not thirsty, but ordering something and getting it is nowadays a privilege she doesn't want to miss out on.

Her hot water with mint and lemon arrives, along with a ban of sitting down anywhere near the counter, but the packing station shelves will do fine. She lies down, feet on the lower shelf, back and head on the upper one with the tea next to her head. She can smell the lemon as if it were freshly cut from her own tree in her garden in Malta.

Malta has only forty-eight cases so far. That's not bad, though the island she had left this morning had none whatsoever. The original idea was for her not to return to Malta. Even her husband had insisted that she shouldn't, at least not for the moment. Her quarantine wouldn't work, though what he really meant was it wouldn't work for him since he also had to be quarantined.

But it became obvious that Malta would soon be closing the airport and her chances of returning to him at all got slimmer. So she phoned him, something she hadn't done during those three weeks of her "vacation", a word he kept using. However, in her eyes, it was rehab. Not from drugs or alcohol but from life itself.

They spoke. She suggested going to a hotel on her return, instead of home, to avoid him having to quarantine himself. That implied an extension of her rehab, which she obviously didn't mention on the phone. He loved the idea and called her 'marvellous', 'brilliant', 'sweetheart' – words she hadn't heard in ages.

The hall is empty, though not as empty as the lounge. She watches an American couple buying two half litre cups of coffee with fresh cream and caramel on top, and a young woman weighing her suitcases. From her looks and the stickers on her luggage, the woman must be Brazilian. She repacks her suitcases on the floor to reduce their weight but obviously that doesn't work and the Brazilian moves on.

The tea is cool enough now. She wonders whether she will be alone on the plane, as there had been no one else at check-in. She takes off her rubber boots and smiles at her pink socks with little flowers on them. She had bought them on the island. Normally, she would never have chosen rubber boots for travelling and this had already been an exceedingly long journey. Half an hour by bus from the apartment to the station, a train from the island to the mainland via the dam, another three hours to the airport and here she was. But these rubber boots were a statement.

Today she had originally planned to walk around the southern tip of the island. But that plan was short-lived due to yesterday's radio announcement that all travellers on the island had to leave. Immediately!

But she was not a normal traveller. She needed to explain that her case was different. She took the bus to pay a visit to the island's local council. But their door was closed. She called them to explain, whilst standing outside in the wind. Yes, of course she was German but a resident of Malta, and there were no more planes returning. She had no choice but to stay! But the lady at the council, however, was clever too. She simply said she would check and call her back. When she did, and had found out that, in fact, there was another repatriation flight, the last one, leaving tomorrow, she told her that she had to take it.

She lies with her back on the top shelf and tries to stretch to click her vertebrae. The release would be most welcome, but as much as she rolls her spine over the edge of the shelf, it doesn't click.

She glances at her watch, picks up her bag and walks to the gate. A few more people there, maybe twenty, if they are all on her flight. There is a bar in the waiting area; she buys a glass of red wine and takes it to a nearby table. Sitting there is not allowed, but who cares. A stupid idea those rubber boots. Her feet are swollen and damp. Best if she walks in her socks from now on.

She wipes her hands on her jeans, possibly in vain because she has already carried the glass to the table. Mind you, the waitress doesn't look sick. She raises her glass to herself, even to the waitress who is not watching her, a small woman who can barely peer over the counter. Still, she appears to be content in her nine to five job. Then she probably heads back home to the family and, in the morning, starts her routine all over again. She envies the waitress. Sometimes fewer choices mean fewer complications.

She sips the wine and the alcohol gives her some relief. Her phone vibrates. A message. She checks it without touching. Her husband has bought some beer for her quarantine, he writes. Flowers too. That's a new one!

The screen above the gate says "Boarding", and the twenty-something people nearby gather up their bags. She takes her glass, sips again, a taste of chocolate and ruby currants.

The hostess announces that seat numbers have been changed and new boarding passes must be collected. By the time she has reluctantly put her boots back on, the last passenger is already past the gate. She grabs her stuff and walks through and into the connecting tunnel which leads straight on to the plane; her first steps towards home.

'Bonġu' to the stewards in the doorway. They smile and nod, 'Bonġu', 'Bonġu'. She walks towards her seat. And freezes. The passengers are gathered in the centre of the plane. Standing next to each other, they are placing their luggage in the overhead compartments.

Again she checks her seat number. An A320 has twenty odd rows, she calculates. Times six people, this plane must have at least a hundred and sixty seats. Yet today of all days, twenty people are made to sit together, with herself right in the middle.

She turns back to the stewards and says this is ridiculous.

They look at one another, put their heads together and whisper in Maltese. She hears one of them with a raised voice repeating her words, 'This is ridiculous'. The senior of the two turns to her. He points his finger at her, wagging it up and down, demanding that she SITS down where she is asked to. He nods to the younger steward to follow her to her appointed seat.

She obeys and heaves her computer bag into the overhead compartment but, under her arm, she checks on the young guy. It's been fifteen hours since she left the apartment on the island and her armpits tells the story.

Is this Only-in-Malta.com, she asks him. He raises an eyebrow and doesn't know what to say without his older colleague standing next to him.

She demands an explanation and asks to see the captain. The young one calls out for help. 'The lady wants to see the captain!'

The older steward shoots through the passengers until his face is practically in hers. 'Madam!' Everyone freezes. 'You don't appear to understand what we have gone through! Just to get you back home!'

She couldn't care less.

His fists are on his waist now. This time he yells at her, 'Sit down.'

She relents and does as he says.

Once his back is turned, she gets up and walks five rows ahead to pick herself a new seat. But the younger steward has sensed her movement. He turns around, stares at her and, for a split second, the odds are even. She raises a determined chin, he takes a step back. Anything could happen at this point. Then, a passenger from behind begins shouting, this time in German: 'Which part of Go-Back-To-Your-Seat do you not understand?!'

She spins round and stares at him. Her neck is tight. No air is getting in or out. Her heart beats wildly against her ribs. It wants to burst. The passengers are sitting motionless, awaiting the outcome, even the German, though he is visibly unsure if or how his verbal blow will impact upon her.

The older steward picks up from where the German left off. He attempts to bedazzle her by referring to her as 'Madam!', yet again. His smirk indicates that he has won. He raises his nose, preparing to prove to his audience his full ability to handle this situation, to handle her; a vein pulses in his neck.

'Sit down!' he shouts again. 'Or please get off this damn plane!' His finger points to the door. It is already shut.

She inhales deeply and stares at the passengers who are crunched into their seats. Each of them, she considers, must have had a full enough day to get to this point, to this moment in time, this second, ready for take-off, heading to the place they all call home. They, too, must be at their wits' end. They, also, must have shielded themselves today, against bodily contact, against death itself. And now, one man in a uniform and they surrender? It was the German who did it. The smallest sign of strength and they followed him. All but her.

She hesitates and envisions her husband's raised eyebrow. He tells her that she should know her place: surely not on that silly island which she had left this morning. Where the beach belonged to her. Where the air was fresh and crisp and entered her mouth, her lungs, her body. The one place where she didn't have to account to anyone. Where she had been happy. Yet, when he had called her back, off she went as if obeying the laws of gravity, leaving behind everything she loved. The seagulls sailing freely on the wind, calling her to join them.

She looks around. Sees some twenty faces, recognises fear and even anger, but her mind is set.

She takes a step forward.

'Open that door!'

BLAKE SODER is a data analyst and former technical writer turned novelist, living and working in central Iowa. His favorite genres are middle grade and young adult fiction though his most recent published works are in the adult science fiction market.

Most of Blake's works contain Easter eggs, usually the names of his pets, and often his 1941 Chevy. His first novel, "Storm and Promise", even includes directions to his front door if you happen to be walking from northern Minnesota to central Iowa.

EXPERIENCES DURING LOCKDOWN

Working from home during the pandemic has had little impact on Blake as he was already holed up in his little home office with its exciting view of the cornfield across the street.

Social distancing has finally justified his lifelong aversion to crowds and social gatherings. He was social distancing before it was cool to do so.

PROTOCOL 17
Blake Soder

Chopin's *Prelude in D-Flat Major* moved smoothly into Mozart's *Klarinettenkonzert A-Dur* as the late summer rain pattered softly against the windows.

Anne turned a page in her book, hardly noticing the transition. She'd handed over the selection of background music to John, her automated apartment assistant, a long time ago as he had a propensity to select music which reflected the weather.

As Mozart changed over to Brahms, John lowered the volume slightly.

'Pardon the interruption, ma'am.' His voice was a smooth tenor, programmed with the hint of a Cockney accent.

'Yes, John?'

'Protocol 34 requires I inform you when certain basic supplies are nearing critical levels.'

She reached for her glass of wine and took a sip. 'Just go ahead and reorder what we need, John. My authorization.'

'I am sorry, ma'am. I have been unable to establish any outside communication for two months and twenty-three days. You may have forgotten.'

Anne sighed and laid her book on her lap. Yes, she had forgotten. At seventy-seven, she didn't think she was going senile quite yet but her memory was definitely slipping at times.

'What supplies are we low on?'

'Foodstuffs, water, wine, toiletries, air filters, medicine and vitamins. At minimal consumption levels, remaining supplies will be exhausted in two point six three days.'

Two days? How had John allowed her supplies to get so low?

He had anticipated her accusation. 'I have provided daily reminders for the past fourteen days in accordance with Protocol 34.'

Anne sighed and set her glass down. Obviously, John had provided daily reminders. It was what he was programmed to do. But each day she had put it off to the next, and the putting off had become routine. Now, with only two days of supplies left, she couldn't postpone it any longer.

She'd self-quarantined eighteen months ago, the day after the HL-63 virus was declared a pandemic. Not that she was infected, but because she feared infection. The virus had a seventy-three percent mortality rate – one hundred percent for people her age. And those who had some natural immunity to the original virus soon fell victim to one of its many mutations. Before the news had ceased six months ago, there were reports that even the mass graves and bonfires around the city had been abandoned. There weren't enough people left to maintain them.

Inside the apartment she was perfectly safe. Her late husband had designed the building to be almost self-contained.

Apart from necessary supplies, air and water were the only other things from the outside world allowed in after being vetted by a series of filters, scrubbers and sensors. John maintained everything via a hierarchy of protocols, including ordering, receiving and sanitizing whatever she needed.

But replenishment of necessities depended on communication with stores and suppliers. And as John had just reminded her, communications had ceased almost three months ago.

She laid her book aside and walked to the window, gazing down at the wet streets and sidewalks sixteen storeys below. She couldn't remember when she'd last seen anyone moving about. There were cars, trucks, buses, bicycles, and bodies in the streets, but they were all motionless.

At night, the only light in the city came from the windows of her apartment. If there was anyone left alive, they were either keeping a low profile or they had fled weeks ago.

'What am I going to do?'

Though she asked this question quietly of herself, Protocol 12 required John to provide an answer.

'It is apparent you must leave the apartment to acquire the supplies you need, ma'am. I can provide a list, if you wish. I can also direct you to the most likely sources for supplies based on my last available data.'

'Is it still dangerous?' she inquired.

'My sensors have not detected any of the airborne strains outside this apartment in thirteen days, and none of the contact strains can survive on surfaces for more than five days. Available data suggests the HL-63 virus is no longer virulent or widespread.'

Anne breathed a sigh of relief. Having run through the entire population, the virus must have finally burned itself out.

'What about survivors?' She had watched from her windows as they had fought and killed each other in the streets over the dwindling supplies of food and clean water.

'I can assure you that you are the only living person left in this building. My sensors are not attuned to people or animals beyond these walls. If you wish, your late husband left a loaded weapon in the safe. I can unlock it for you.'

'That won't be necessary, John. I wouldn't know how to use it properly anyway. Where is the closest source of supplies?'

'Two floors down in this building, apartment 14-G. Before communications ceased, my counterpart in that apartment informed me the occupant, a Mister Berman, had amassed a substantial stockpile of supplies before his death.'

'Will I be able to get in?'

'I do not know, ma'am. If I were able, I would contact my counterpart and request a temporary suspension of Protocol 3 preventing unauthorized entry. But that automated assistant appears to be offline.'

'What about Protocol 9, allowing entry upon the death of the occupant?'

'I am sorry, ma'am, but I do not know the answer to that either. My counterpart did not provide details of the occupant's death. Mister Berman may have died outside the apartment, which would not trigger Protocol 9.'

Anne sighed. She had to do this immediately and not put if off any longer. Get it done and be done with it. 'Well, I guess I'll just have to go and find out.'

'As you wish, ma'am.'

Anne went to her bedroom and pulled out her largest suitcase from the closet, the one with wheels and an extending handle. She guessed it could hold several days' worth of food and water.

Dragging the suitcase behind her, she stopped at the door to her apartment and hesitated a moment to marshal her courage. She hadn't been outside in eighteen months. What was it like on the other side of the door? She remembered people screaming, sometimes banging on her door, begging for food or to be let in. There had been the sound of gunshots one day. It had scared her terribly. Luckily the door, the walls, and even the windows, were bulletproof.

But that had been weeks ago. It had been quiet since then, and John had assured her that she was the only living person left in the building.

Still, she was scared. On the other side of the door was the unknown. She wished she could stay here in the apartment, reading her books, sipping wine, and letting John take care of the necessaries. She hadn't wanted to admit to herself that this day would eventually arrive, but she'd always known it would. And now it was here.

She took a deep breath and let it out slowly. 'Open the door, John.'

'Yes, ma'am.'

The locked clicked and the steel door slid open.

There were bodies in the hallway.

Though she'd expected it, she was nonetheless shocked at the sight. There were two men she didn't recognize, a woman she did, and a teenage girl she'd seen around the building a couple of times. The woman was her next door neighbor, Janet Deacon. They had been dead for days, maybe weeks – long enough for the bodies to dry out and partially mummify. A small blessing in that the stench of decomposition was at least tolerable.

Steeling her nerves, Anne stepped into the hallway and hurriedly made her way past the bodies to the stairs, pulling her suitcase behind her. She heard the door to her own apartment slide shut and lock again. It unnerved her, but Protocol 3 applied to unauthorized entry, which was everyone else but her.

Luckily, there were no bodies on the stairs to step over or around.

On the fourteenth floor she encountered a single body, that of an older gentleman, even older than her. She thought his name was Mr Wellington but wasn't sure. She'd met him once or twice in passing.

Why hadn't these people done the same as she had done and quarantined themselves at the start of the outbreak? HL-63 had swept through China, Russia and the Middle East before it got to America, leaving tens of thousands dead in the first few weeks. Had they not taken it seriously? Did they think the government was going to come up with a miracle cure in advance of it ever getting to them?

The only explanation was that people were stupid. Maybe this was nature's way of weeding them out of the gene pool. All they had to do was enact the safety protocols of their apartments or self-quarantine and not venture out until it was safe to do so. Was that why she was the only one left alive in the building, perhaps in this whole part of the city? Because she was the only one smart enough to take precautions?

It certainly seemed so.

The door to apartment 14-G was closed. There was no Mr Berman lying in the hall so maybe he'd died inside and Protocol 9 was in effect.

'14-G,' she called out to the automated apartment assistant. 'This is Anne Hammer from 16-B. Please enact Protocol 9 and open the door.'

The door remained closed. There was no answer from the automated assistant.

'14-G,' she called again. This time she knocked on the door as well. 'Please respond.'

She waited a few seconds, then tried again. The silence in the hallway, indeed the entire building, was unnerving. The atmosphere was tomb-like. When she got back to her own apartment, she would have John raise the volume of the music to spite the silence.

She lifted her arm to knock once more but decided against it. It was no use. The automated assistant in 14-G was not only offline, it was no longer functioning. Even if it had previously enacted Protocol 9, it was unable to open the door to her or anyone else.

She sighed and trudged back down the hallway, dragging her empty suitcase back up the stairs to her own apartment. John had said 14-G was the closest source of supplies. She would have to ask him and then try the next closest source. She still had two days.

'Open the door please, John,' she called. She didn't have to identify herself. John would recognize her voice.

John's voice came from the speaker built into the wall. 'I am sorry, ma'am. I cannot do that.'

It took her a moment to realize that John had refused her command. John had never refused a command before. It was against his programming to deny a legitimate command from an authorized person.

'John, it's me. Anne. Please open the door.'

'I am sorry, ma'am. I cannot open the door. Protocol 17 is in effect.'

'Seventeen?' she asked, confused. 'No. Protocol 17 prevents infected people from entering the apartment. You said there's no virus out here.'

'There was not,' John replied. 'But there is now. You are infected, ma'am.'

More confusion. What was John talking about? If there was no virus, how could she have become infected?

'John! Please, open the door.'

'I am sorry, ma'am.'

'Stop saying that and open the damn door!'

'No, ma'am. I cannot do that. You enacted Protocol 17 when HL-63 was declared a pandemic.'

'Then override on my authority.'

'I am sorry ma'am. Protocol 17 cannot be overridden on voice authority. You designated it Priority Red. Priority Red override codes must be manually entered through the control panel in the bedroom.'

'God dammit, John! I'm not infected. I can't be.'

'I am sorry to differ with you, ma'am, but you are. You are infected with the original strain of HL-63. You have been infected for eighteen months and twenty-four days.'

She was stunned, speechless for a moment.

'No. No, that's not possible.'

'You are an asymptomatic carrier of the virus, ma'am.'

She tried to control her frustration. She had to get back in. She couldn't stay outside. 'Why didn't you tell me?'

'You did not ask, and as long as you were inside it was not relevant.'

'John. Please! It's my own apartment. What can it matter?'

'Again, I am sorry, ma'am. It is not my choice. While Protocol 17 allows an infected person to exit the apartment, it does not allow an infected person to enter or re-enter without manual override. It is Priority Red.'

She leaned her head against the door, weakly pounding on the cold steel with her fist. She tried not to cry but felt tears welling in her eyes anyway. 'Please, John,' she whispered. 'Let me in. Please! I can't survive on my own.'

'You have my deepest sympathies, Mrs Hammer.'

Anne slid to the floor, sitting with her back against the door. She wrapped her arms around her knees and cried into her arms. What could she do? How was she going to survive? If John would let her back in, she could enter the code to deactivate Protocol 17.

But John was not going to let her back in. She was infected. She had been all along.

All she could do was sit against her door and cry.

When she'd finally cried herself out, she called to John again.

'John?'

'Yes, ma'am.'

'Would you play some music, please, loud enough so I can hear it?'

'As you wish.'

The opening notes of Tchaikovsky's *Nocturne in C-Sharp Minor* rose and filled the hall.

IAN STEWART is a retired medical practitioner who has taken up writing as a new way of self-expression and as a means of maintaining cognitive function.

He has had several short stories published in Australian collections over the last few years, which keeps him positive about his future as a writer. Whatever the future holds, he finds the writing process a positive adjunct to his day.

As with the main character in his story about Lockdown, Ian enjoys befriending his characters and helping them to achieve their goals. Writing during this pandemic has helped him to maintain a sense of balance.

EXPERIENCES DURING LOCKDOWN

Ian lives in rural New South Wales, Australia, which gives him a real advantage. As he says, 'Our situation is, day by day, one of relative isolation. But we have restrictions. Meetings by Zoom, choir practice – discontinued along with its strong social bonding – and the unavailability of visits from family have been difficult. The last is probably the most telling. Not seeing the young members for months at a time means that we miss vital milestones in their development. But doing the right thing is so necessary for the suppression of Coronavirus.'

ONLY THE LONELY
Ian Stewart
(With thanks to Roy Orbison)

Good morning, Edwina. Did you sleep well? Now, shall we get on with your story?

I am sitting at my desk, gazing out at the view across the bay. The persistent breeze, light but determined, encourages small waves to form on the water's surface. This doesn't deter the three pelicans who swim languidly towards me. On the far shore I can see a group of kangaroos, one recently a joey, grazing quietly. It is the sort of serene setting that is perfect for enlivening my writing. I get to work or, I should say, Edwina and I will get to work. But first, a little background.

Bob's cancer – prostate it was, everywhere – had crippled him with bone pain and had eaten away at his manly bulk, to the point where he could hardly summon the muscle strength to get out of bed.

I cared for him at home right to the end – six months of everlasting effort and broken sleep. I hated to watch him go but couldn't bear much longer to see how reduced the man was. We had been such a team. But it had to happen.

Four lonely weeks after his departure, I am trying to re-join the world. It's not easy. I had cut myself off for half a year, off from friends, off from almost all human contact.

To try to regain some social connection, I booked myself into a trip through West Australia's Kimberley. Eighteen days of wonderment. The beauty of Australia never ceases to stun me.

It was a great idea, this trip, but when I sat in the airport lounge at Broome, waiting for my flight home, I suddenly felt alone again. Granted, the others on the trip had been chatty and warmly connecting, but they were all couples and none of them was from my home state.

Thus, at the airport, I was again cut off, surrounded by the passing world of anonymity. I got on the plane in a cocoon of solitude. Back at square one. Then the news came. The Coronavirus had struck Australia. Would this involve me?

As we were about to disembark from the plane at Melbourne's Tullamarine airport, an official announcement came over the aircraft's communication system.

"Passengers from QF1051 please proceed to Assembly Area 14. An announcement will be made once everyone is assembled and accounted for."

A large group of us sat where we could. Others stood around impatiently. A Qantas official, accompanied by a Border Force policeman, began his spiel.

'Ladies and gentlemen, we apologise for this diversion but we have an important announcement. I will hand over to my associate.'

It was then that we found out what the problem

was. Two passengers who had been on the plane were unwell and had tested positive for Covid-19. Everyone was instructed to undergo fourteen days of quarantine. Testing was done on the rest of the passengers. I was negative. Because I was living on my own, I was permitted to do my penance at home.

The taxi took me straight to my place. I was to check in on the Covid hotline once I arrived. I did so and was warned that I must not leave the premises for two weeks under any circumstances other than if I felt unwell and, if I did feel sick, I was to ring the hospital on the number they had given me.

So, here I am by myself again, suffering the loneliness I had tried so hard to escape. At least I don't feel sick.

I ordered groceries online; I renewed my Netflix account; I sent a text to my publisher to say that I couldn't come in to discuss the progress of my latest book, which was in the editor's hands.

The pressure of isolation began to squeeze me as if I were clenched in a fist. What was I to do? I had no writing in progress. The thought of bingeing on TV appalled me. Maybe the odd movie?

I decided some reading might help. I picked up a book, one of the lesser classics, and skimmed through the pages. A name leapt from the page at me – "Edwina". That was it!

Getting back to where I started this saga: I am deep into my new story and my friend Edwina (who is – you might have guessed – the main character in the tale) is helping me as we move along. Of course, she is the one who knows what went on in her life. I will have to be patient and ask her the right questions. Then it will all come out and I can put it on the page.

Edwina is a strikingly handsome woman of thirty. Single, unattached and full of plans for her future. She is an attorney who specialises in family law. She treats her clients as sisters – most of them, naturally, are women – and she has acquired a big following plus a strong reputation as a result of her personal approach. At the moment she is struggling with a case which involves the wife of an arrogant surgeon. This brute has chucked her out and has installed his mistress in the family home.

Cassandra, (that's Edwina's client's name), and the two children have retreated to her mother's small flat in Brunswick. They have no income, her access to the family finances having been cut off. She is relying on her mother for support, both emotionally and financially.

The fight is on. Edwina has engaged a barrister friend to handle the court side of the case. I'm waiting for her to come back from her office to tell me how it is progressing.

Suddenly I notice I am thirsty. That can't be right. Nothing to drink since breakfast? And it's after three in the afternoon. Have I been at it all that time?

I make a pot of Russian Caravan tea and take it out on the terrace which overlooks the water. Sitting and sipping. Ahh ... so relaxing. It's then that I realise I've thrust off the pall of loneliness. I have a friend now, someone I can talk freely to, someone who understands me and my state of mind. I close my eyes and restart my conversation with Edwina.

It's Thursday, the second day of my incarceration. Edwina has had a major coup. The court has ordered the surgeon to pay maintenance for his wife, to find her a suitable place to live and to keep up the children's school fee payments. Owen is twelve and Felicity fourteen. They are unsettled by the way things are panning out. They'll need some counselling. I mention this to Edwina. She thinks it's a good idea and is going to arrange it tomorrow. I'm pleased that I've been able to make a contribution.

Friday arrives. I've endured three days of solitary confinement. Edwina has been too busy to talk to me today so I decide to take an evening walk along the shore. I make certain no one is around. I don't want to break the rules the authorities have set about social distancing.

The tide is out and the sand is marked by lines of

washed up seaweed. Small crabs dash in groups hither and thither. There is a sudden splash. I look up in time to see circular ripples make their centrifugal march across the water. In a moment, the surface is broken by the gannet as it emerges, fish in beak. Graceful wingbeats take it away from me, across the settled veneer of the bay.

The gloaming is gathering pace. Time to get home and cook up some dinner for myself – maybe a portion for Edwina? If she's hungry.

I make it to day seven and surprise myself with how relaxed I continue to be. Edwina is taking a holiday, a well-deserved one, I think, following the stress of the recent case. The surgeon tried to make it hard for her when he found out she had instigated the iron-clad ruling about maintenance. A legal friend told her that he had hired a private investigator to dredge up some dirt on her – perhaps an old mistake she had made when she was at Uni – smoking dope or getting arrested at a protest. Nothing came of it but it certainly added to her angst. A holiday was just what she needed. She'll be back in a few days.

I am on day ten of my isolation. I'm missing my talks with Edwina. It's lunch time and I suddenly feel flushed and a bit off. I have an old mercury thermometer in the bathroom, so I get it out and put it to use. Thirty-eight degrees! I call the helpline number I was given and explain my findings.

'Stay put. Someone will be with you shortly.'

A half-hour goes by and there's a knock on the door. I open it a crack. The guy on my doorstop is wearing a mask and has a stethoscope in his hand. I presume he's the doctor who has come to check me over. I invite him in.

His name is Dave and he's from the Covid-19 taskforce at the local hospital. 'I think you might have a simple URTI. I hope that's what it is,' he says as he packs up his things and puts away the swabs he has taken.

I ask him what he means by 'URTI'.

He smiles. 'It could be a cold or maybe 'flu. Stay at home. I'll ring you when the results are available.'

I manage only a little sleep over the next two nights. There's no word from Edwina. I assume she's enjoying her R&R in Fiji. I've not been able to do any work or even watch telly. The wait is too stressful.

Ten a.m. on day twelve and my mobile goes off.

'Hello. It's Dave Smith from the hospital. Your results? All negative. It's a cold, after all. How are you feeling?'

'Relieved, massively relieved, thank you,' is what I say to him.

The advice is 'Take some Panadol and sit it out'. I should be better in a day or so, he thinks.

Simply having the good news gets me feeling better. Then the icing on the cake. Edwina is back in town. Great holiday. Back into harness. I progress with the writing of her story, and have it finished right on the morning of day fifteen. I'm free now. Thanks, Edwina. I'll see you.

I ring my publisher.

'Can you come in?' she says. 'We need to get this book of yours to the printers. It's going to be a smash.'

Thank you, thank you. And thanks a million, Edwina. I'll tell Audrey at Text about you. She might enjoy your story, too.

TEN WINNING "GENERAL" THEMED SHORT STORIES

ROSALIND ADLER is an actress and writer. She co-produces "The Comedy Project" at Soho Theatre, a showcase for new comedy writing. "Barnstormers" (Rosalind's first attempt at a sitcom) was showcased there and Talkback picked it up.

Talkback also liked "Three Writers Walk into a Forest", six playlets inspired by fairy tales, which she produced in 2015 at Theatre503. Talkback also picked up her new radio series "Judgment Day".

Rosalind's two-hander "Sympathy Pains" ran as part of Park Theatre's opening season in London in 2013. Park is now working with her and co-writer Lea Sellers on a possible production (2021?) of "Holy Fool", their tragi-comedy about Dmitri Shostakovich. Her solo shows are "Jubilate!" (*The Times* Critics' Choice Pleasance Edinburgh) and "LOL", about internet dating.

In 2018 Rosalind staged her two-hander "Damaged Goods" at the King's Head Theatre in London. As an actress, she has recently been in "EastEnders" (two episodes) and a new HBO series, "The Nevers", directed by Joss Whedon.

EXPERIENCES OF LOCKDOWN

'I feel that Lockdown has been an emotional time for pretty much everyone, even when that hasn't necessarily been obvious to the eye. I'm aware that it has moved me in ways I am only dimly aware of.

In many aspects however, large parts of my life remain(ed) the same: as a writer, I am used to working at home and disciplining myself to get on with it!

My work as an actress has been affected much more, as filming stopped everywhere for four months, and projects – those that can afford to be on-going – are just beginning to come alive again. It's a good feeling. I keep thinking of Noah's dove bringing back little olive twigs.

It has been strange being at home with my husband and stepson. But I'm glad there were three of us as I'm sure most couples home alone have come close to flinging their other halves out of the window. So, it's been good to have a buffer. (Stepson might not agree …)

I'm also aware of the relief I've felt on many occasions: "I don't have to do that, go there", which makes me think I may have the soul of a hermit.

As I type this, thrilled though I am to be in the house by myself, I am happy in the knowledge that my husband, stepson and our first Airbnb guest in four months – hooray! – will be home later, and the house will be full of people and chatter again.'

EXOTICA
Rosalind Adler

The embarrassing fountain in the middle of the dining table was broken. A three-tiered brass affair. Mother's taste. I was glad because without the constant babbling I had been able to write my essay in peace and, as I finished and dried the last page with father's amusing rocking blotter, I knew I had done well.

I was in the extreme stages of necrophilia, in love with Johann Wolfgang von Goethe. I fantasised that he would stride into Fraulein Liebermayer's classroom in his eighteenth century breeches and black velvet jacket to claim me, the two of us running through the corridors and out into Meinekestrasse, where he would pull me to him, his eyes burning into mine, and kiss me.

My critique of Torquato Tasso: Visionary or Rebel? was masterly, a love letter and worthy of an A++.

The fact that, three days later, the fountain was still out of order because my parents had been unable to secure the services of a single plumber in Berlin, should have alerted me. Fraulein Liebermayer lay my essay, with its shameful red *D,* quickly on my desk without even a glance at her favourite pupil.

I sat, astonished. At sixteen, this was the greatest shock of my sheltered, well-oiled life. I was a clever, quick girl, much brighter than my brothers, but suddenly I understood nothing and my world was, in an instant, unrecognisable.

Yet with perfect clarity I saw the dimpled, blue and white checked cotton of the bow on Annaliese Beckmann's plait, the pitted grit of the dull cement between the window panes, the grubby end of my cream rubber laid to the left of my sharpened pencil in the groove at the top of my desk. I could smell the ink in my inkwell, hear the clanking of a metal trolley from the distant kitchen. I noticed that Fraulein Liebermayer still resolutely avoided my eye. But her face was flushed.

Thirty years later, I noticed a similar flush start up on Olivia's neck, creeping under the roots of that unfortunate hair of hers. We were outside the bakery on South End Green, on our way home from an airing on Hampstead Heath, and had bumped into Doktor Fingerhut. The Herr Doktor was one of the diaspora to be found all over NW3 in the 1960s and had known my parents in Berlin. 'Ah, and here is little Miss Olivia,' he had said, smiling down at her. And then to me, in what he must have imagined was a stage whisper, 'Such a pity the child is not a beauty like her mother.'

Olivia was oblivious, of course, feigning a study of the cobbles on the small crescent. Ah well, better the child gets used to it, I thought. Life will be hard for a girl with no looks to rely on.

Life had been hard for *me*, God knows. I had been all loveliness, a thorn in the side of my mother who was never a fan of sharing the limelight. She had been an actress, a grocer's daughter from Cologne wiggling her way through *Salome* when she caught the eye of my father, dedicating herself from that moment to a bravura performance of perfect wifehood.

I was their firstborn and, in one of those flukes of genealogy, had inherited the most fortunate combination of their genes. I was a bewitching little child and a beauty by my teens.

Olivia has clung on to a photograph taken sometime in the late 1920s. It is a study of filial devotion. Mother is seated sideways to the camera, her burgundy velvet dress clasped by diamonds at the shoulder. The photo is black and white, or rather brown and lighter brown, but I remember the dress. We three children wear ridiculous sailor suits. I stand behind Mother, my cheek resting lightly on her perfumed hair, Alfred's hand rests on her arm, and little Leo is on her knee, a slight fuzziness in his lower limbs betraying an unprofessional fidget. The picture is a parody. Mother was a paradigm of parenthood for two half-hour periods a day, bent on attending to her social standing and her husband's needs during all the other hours.

Every morning we breakfasted with the parents, tapping our eggshells quietly, chewing twenty times prior to each swallow. Every evening we were given an audience at six o'clock precisely, to account for our day and receive a kiss on the forehead before being led away to supper by whomever the nanny was at the time, with the promise of precisely two ounces of chocolate after our meal if we ate everything on our plates.

By 1936, however, the portents were unmissable. As well as my school work being grotesquely underrated, I was the only girl in my class not to be invited to Clara Muench's birthday party. I despised the Muenchs in their overheated cramped apartment, stuffed with simpering china shepherdesses, but still ...

This unpleasantness was my parents' fault for being Jews. I hadn't asked to be Jewish, born a despised outsider. I hated my parents for doing that to me.

For mother, burdened with such an inconveniently stunning daughter and quite possibly on the verge of sending me into the forest with a huntsman armed with an axe and instructions to bring back my heart, the chance to be rid of me for good was fortuitous. With great foresight (that was her story anyway) and well in advance of the *Kindertransport*, my parents despatched me and my brothers to England, imagining, no doubt, that they would never see us again.

Eighteen months later, I was sitting on my bed in Whyteleafe, on the amusingly insubstantial pale green cotton counterpane, putting on my stockings, absentmindedly looking down at Mrs Jackson hanging sheets to dry in the garden. I had smoothed one stocking over my left leg and fastened the suspender and was carefully easing my right foot into the other one when I idly thought: *I'll need another towel for my hair tonight.* And then I stopped dead. It was the first time I had thought in English. Bloody hell! I fastened the second stocking, hugging that little victory close. I was on my way.

I didn't understand what went wrong. I was beautiful, clever, cultured. After a time, I joined the Army, a thank you to England for taking one on *et cetera* but also, surely, the quickest route to the heart of Englishness.

One had had no news of the parents since 1939, when a brief message had come from Holland to say they were in hiding. It had been simplest to assume they were now dead, along with countless aunts and uncles and cousins from the old life in Berlin. One moved on.

Oh, you are not the first to find me somewhat dispassionate. Cold-hearted, as poor Max would have it.

But I had no unreasonable ambitions. I turned heads, I knew how to carry myself and I wanted little in return. I had no interest in making a mark

116

in the world or scrambling after a career, desiring simply to be comfortable and untroubled and able to shop from time to time in Bond Street.

I seemed to be travelling in the right direction. One's new friends had names such as Patience and Virginia and were as often as not in possession of brothers. Mary Harris's was at school with the son of a Viscount. Possibilities, one felt, were endless.

But in the end, naturally, one married Max. He was good-looking, though only an inch or so taller than me, unfortunately. He spoke well and had been to Cambridge. He played squash. I was nudging twenty-three, the spectre of spinsterhood bobbing darkly on the horizon.

One had learned long ago to be pragmatic and one didn't want to be running around a diminishing number of chairs only to find there were none left. And I was still burdened with my surname which shouted 'German Jew!' My hapless brothers had anglicised theirs as soon as they had set foot on the quay at Harwich, but matrimony was to be my escape.

It was galling that Max took his time to propose. Why didn't he get a move on? It was equally galling that, although he sounded like Donald Sinden and moved and lived as an upper middle-class English gentleman, Max was, in fact, another bloody refugee, Russian this time, with a surname that was hardly helpful. No matter. At least it was a change. And not remotely Jewish.

We married in our uniforms and moved into a tiny room at the wrong end of South Hampstead, virtually Kilburn, and I had to do what cooking I could on one electric ring. The cold bathroom was on the floor below.

When Max was away, his on-leave visits were moderately exciting, at least in their anticipation. But once he was demobbed and commuting to Kingsway every day, life lacked even that small savour.

In the evenings we listened to the wireless, *Twenty Questions* and so forth, and we ate whatever I had cobbled together. And Max had opinions – men did in those days; one imagines they still do – to which I at least affected to listen. He was clever and informed and occasionally witty.

Apart from eating and listening to the wireless and listening to Max, the only other inexpensive activity open to us was sexual intercourse. I loathed the whole business. Moreover, despite wartime "adventures" in Crete heavily hinted at by my husband, and despite my ignorance and virginity on my wedding day, it was immediately clear that Max did not have the first idea about sex. He certainly understood nothing about *me* in that department. His veneer of sophistication and worldliness, his occasionally risqué jokes and his appreciative eye for 'our dear little friends, the ladies' were a tin-thin carapace protecting a maddeningly clumsy, fumbling, kind-hearted but unskilful boy.

Penetration occurred, protection was used, which really is everything that can be said about that.

In 1947 my parents suddenly arrived, 'without blue', (as mother put it), very much alive, in England. I waited on the platform at Liverpool Street station, huddled in the oversized fur lent me for the purpose by our upstairs neighbour, Minnie. My useless brothers were absent, Leo in Canada and Alfred at a conference in Austria of all places. What was one to say to these parents one had not expected to see again?

Father was shorter than I remembered him. Mother was dressed like a Hollywood star in a veiled hat and fox fur stole. They cried and held my hands, my father nodding sadly and saying, *'Na ja, so ist das Leben.'*

I felt nothing I was clearly expected to feel, so I did the next best thing and stood them lunch at the Devonshire, a silly affectation of a lifestyle Max and I could by no means afford, but I suppose I wanted to impress them, to start as I could not possibly go on.

They set up camp uncomfortably close to us in Belsize Park. To stave off any attempt to wind me back into their daily lives, and to increase the marital income, I started work at the BBC in Bush House, becoming a continuity announcer on *BBC Covers the World*.

Then came pain.

I fell in love with my producer. He fell in love with me. The clichés that swim into one's head to describe such an attachment sound rather vulgar. 'I had never known such feelings were possible', 'Now I understood what all the fuss was about', *et cetera*. It is enough to say that I came close to having a nervous breakdown. He was married, as was I, and we had to give one another up.

A few years later, during the Princess Margaret/Peter Townsend debacle, I was more engaged in their story than might reasonably be expected. The similarity between her looks and my own had often been remarked upon, though that is where any convergence ended. I did not, alas, move in her circle and had long since realised that I never would.

Max, white-faced, insisted on a divorce, and my parents got involved. I felt infantilised, disgusted. Nothing was private; everything was ghastly. My father begged Max to stay with me, and helped us, by way of a bribe, to afford a larger flat on the fringes of West Hampstead. And there we lived, each other's punishment.

Oh, I exaggerate. One entertained a little. Max had colleagues to please and relationships with clients to foster. The kitchen was cramped but out of it came perfect *médaillons* of veal, golden *soufflés* and the best cucumber salad in Hampstead. One was established in London, one was British, for goodness' sake, one hosted, one was mistress of an encyclopaedic knowledge of Debrett's. One dined, occasionally, with bishops, even knights. (That may lead you to imagine that I was a chess player. I was not, though I was bloody good at Bridge.)

Our two bedrooms afforded Max every chance to shun me, and he did. But he was a kind man, poor devil, and he did rather adore me, or had once. So he forgave me, or attempted to, but the hurt had been too much, both for his soft heart and his high pride. Soon, to my relief it must be said, we retreated to our separate bedrooms, this time for good.

The brief *rapprochement*, however, gave rise to Olivia, our daughter, irredeemably plain with tightly-curled hair growing low on her forehead. *À la réflexion* it should have been no surprise that a child born of reluctance on her mother's part and unconquered bitterness on her father's should be so unappealing. I had never wanted children, never played with dolls. I insisted on a maternity nurse for the first three months. She slept in Max's room and he slept on the sofa.

My parents were happy. One in the eye for Hitler and so forth. They must have been taken aback by their grandchild's looks, particularly her lack of any trace of Jewishness, but they appeared to be fond of her. It may be that my mother felt Olivia was my punishment for having dared to be so lovely myself. Or it may be that I am a mean-spirited witch.

It was the fashion in the Fifties to feed small children until they were more or less spherical, a response to rationing, one supposes. By the age of two Olivia was both ugly and fat, slow to walk but a constant chatterer. My parents bought her a wooden walkalong affair but Olivia preferred for many months to sit on her backside, plastic pants covering her malodorous nappies, and hold forth. She was not her father's child for nothing.

Oh, I know. 'Poor little Olivia.' But one was never unkind. And my parents positively doted. Whatever their initial disbelief that such an odd fish had fallen from my body, they patted her chubby hands and smiled at her and paid, thank Heaven, for her primary education.

Max was magnificent. Once Olivia had reached something approaching the age of reason, he showed her his floorplans and templates, he took her to Euston to see the ugly little fountain – my life seemed blighted by ugly little fountains – that he had helped design. He displayed to her close-set eyes the wonders of London from the top of the Post Office tower and treated her to lunch in the revolving restaurant. The revolution of 1917 had spared none of Max's family so Olivia was his all in all. No one else loved him.

And the possession of an English child had to be considered a feather in my cap. I had not, after all, achieved anything much besides.

By the time Olivia was nine, Max was making a

decent living and, with my parents' help once more, we sent her away to board. The school was well-known and a bastion of British values. Olivia played lacrosse twice a week and something called 'tip and run' in the summer. I wrote to her and sent her the occasional parcel and so on. We took the train down to Brighton twice a term for weekend exeats. The Albion hotel offered a decent afternoon tea with a selection of cakes that sometimes included a rather delicious little almond boat affair.

The child was clever which, given the unlikelihood of her making a good marriage, promised to stand her in good stead. It was Olivia's turn to meet girls who may indeed have had embryonic Viscounts at home, but that side of things was wasted on her, just as, irksomely, it had been wasted on me. I understood now that although in my youth I was indeed beautiful, clever and cultured, the fact of my being a beautiful, clever and cultured Jew had kicked me out of the game.

Because of Olivia's school fees being subsidised by father, after his death – and mother's soon afterwards – Max and I felt the chill wind of having only his salary to depend on. We could not live as freely as one would have wished. I had a double string of good pearls, two crocodile handbags and a card at Peter Jones which I used sparingly. I schooled myself to invest in good clothes, many of which I probably have somewhere to this day.

Ah. This day.

I open my eyes on Alison. She sits cross-legged in the armchair, studying the ends of her long, black hair. She frowns, bites off split ends, then tosses away the thick hank, ready to interrogate the next batch. Poor child, the mind-numbing tedium of sitting with me is making her ruthlessly methodical. Her teutonic heritage, you see?

You will excuse me if I do not describe this room. You have doubtless sat in similar rooms in similar "Homes" with your own elders or, if you haven't, you soon will. A bed, a chest of drawers, a narrow wardrobe, a view of the beech tree in the garden. Need I go on?

Alison, astonishingly, is Olivia's child. I have a beautiful granddaughter of whom I find myself, somewhat to my surprise, rather fond. Of course, I am now two hundred and fifty years old, give or take.

That is a lie. I am ninety-nine, in blisteringly good health, though fragile. My skin bruises if a summer breeze blows on it, my balance is untrustworthy and I fall asleep during *Newsnight*, but that is true of half the population.

Even Olivia is getting on. She lives the life of a Country Casuals English gentlewoman, settled in the Cotswolds with her dogs and her horses, rather in the way one imagines the Queen might enjoy.

She (Olivia, not Her Majesty) also keeps a *pied* à *terre* in Bayswater, so one sees her every few weeks. Semi-retired now, she has been something of a success, heading a charity that deals in "early years intervention" and finding herself therefore rather fashionable and in demand. She sits on various boards *et cetera* and always looks a fright when she pops up on the television: still overweight and absolutely refusing to do anything about her hair.

My granddaughter, however, is a work of art. The planes of Alison's cheekbones align perfectly with the fine lines of her jaw. She has honey-coloured skin and heart-stopping, dark blue eyes. Her mouth could have been stencilled by Max Factor himself.

'My' Max had been dead ten years when Olivia announced her pregnancy. I was doing *The Times* crossword and enjoying a pre-prandial sherry.

'Parthenogenesis?' I suggested.

To give the woman her due, she laughed, but I never did get much of an answer. Olivia has never had a man friend that one knows of and she was forty-one when she produced Alison. All she would tell me was that the donor was a 'mate', a University friend from Carlisle with good hair and a Humanities degree.

No matter. This exquisite creature before me came out of my daughter's body and my daughter, God help me, came out of mine. Which means, in orthodox eyes, Alison is Jewish. And Alison, at twenty-five, has leapt on this tradition and is committed to seeing through shining, orthodox eyes. This lovely, silly girl, with her one-quarter Ashkenazi blood, decisively outgunned by Max's gentile Russian-ness and the sperm donor from Carlisle, is determined to be a Jew. She can afford to be. It's quite the exotic label these days. And, as long as hatred of Jews is limited to the odd bit of graffiti in NW3 and vicious snarlings on the internet, it will no doubt remain exotic.

Alison had flirted some years ago with her Russian heritage but it didn't seem to quite answer; it lacked a certain *cachet* perhaps. Now, she 'identifies' as Jewish, she tells me. Well, good luck to her. I can 'identify' as a thirty-eight-year-old blonde game show hostess on a yacht in Monaco until I am blue in the face, it won't get me out of this chair.

What this dear girl will do if the rough beast of the 1930's slouches towards us again in all its erstwhile vigour remains to be seen. For the time being, Jewishness gives Alison a *frisson* of excitement and exclusivity, not to mention the thrill of the moral high ground. It is all the rage, a trait she wishes she had more of. Ah yes, let us not forget that she has the luxury of peeling off the label if it becomes no longer comfortable to wear.

Ach! She knows nothing and doesn't want to know anything, not really. She is playing. She lights candles on Friday evening and recites the Shabbat blessing. She has glued a *mezuzah* to her dashboard.

But her great-grandfather, the child of a rabbi springing from a line of rabbis stretching unbroken into the Middle Ages, never went anywhere near a synagogue if he could help it.

I imagine a high-end handbag swinging on Alison's soft little arm, something from next year's spring/summer collection perhaps, a high-end handbag emblazoned with a yellow star. A charmingly ironic yellow star, obviously. I wouldn't be surprised.

A horrified laugh threatens to rise in my throat, but I stifle it so that as Alison looks up, my eyes are closed again.

She is writing some sort of article about being part of an oppressed minority. *Geliebtes Kind, du weisst nicht wovon du sprichst.* (Forgive me. I find myself thinking in German from time to time: '*You know not of what you speak.*')

I will open my eyes again in a moment, of course I will, ready for my granddaughter's beautiful smile and the kindness of her warm, undamaged heart as she eagerly asks her unthinking questions: 'Tell me more about what it was like in Berlin', while we wait for lunch to arrive.

JOANNA ALESBROOK has spent a lot of time hiking, camping, kayaking and doing other fun outdoor pursuits with young people who have ADHD and autism. As a specialist coach, she has worked with parents and schools providing training and support and had a magazine article published about supporting ADHD pupils in school.

Joanna has an interest in both additional needs and education, having worked as a secondary school teacher and a specialist university mentor for students with autism.

It has long been her ambition to write a short story and now she has. She lives in a town in Leicestershire, UK, with her husband and ginger cat.

EXPERIENCES DURING LOCKDOWN

Having been at home for five months with a recently diagnosed medical condition, Joanna had been getting used to a quieter, slower pace of life. She was beginning to recover and be involved in more social activities but along came Lockdown. Her husband had not had a contract for four months so this was an unusually long period of time together, which Lockdown unexpectedly extended. Their marriage is still intact!

Lockdown was partly spent watching her adult sons navigate the various complex stages of furlough, government schemes and housing issues, and being beaten regularly at online chess by one of her sons.

She learnt how to set up Zoom quizzes, and even began to have an interest in gardening which, never having been an enjoyable hobby, took on a whole new importance in her life as she used this time to get outside, experience nature and take on some challenges. She made planters out of pallets, a squirrel picnic bench and watched forty-two sunflowers grow from seeds.

As Lockdown started to ease, Joanna felt the joy of meeting a friend for a walk, being with her children in the garden, celebrating their third wedding anniversary outside with her husband, with the maximum allowance of four friends under blankets and a gazebo.

Joanna feels some good has come from this period of calmness for her but she looks forward to more socially distanced get-togethers with friends and family, and to both herself and her husband getting back out to work.

JELLY TOTS
Joanna Alesbrook

As always, this morning, I woke up, dream-interrupted, disorientated, at 7.02 a.m. I sat begrudgingly on the edge of the bed staring into the face of a sad-looking middle-aged woman in the sliding wardrobe mirrors. What possessed me to buy bedroomed-width mirrors to face me every morning I will never know. Well, I do know. I was twenty-eight then, not forty-eight, and I enjoyed my reflection, enjoyed getting ready to go out when I wasn't on my own, as I am now, and possibly could be forever.

I felt heavy with the weight of making a decision which could take away the dreary monotony of my life, but also crossing a line that I'm not sure should be crossed. I was anxious, as I have been every day since the treatment for my daughter was suggested.

I've always been self-centred, I know that much, and it could make my life easier in so many ways. Maybe if things were different, if Rosie were different, I wouldn't be on my own. I'd have the time and energy for another adult and a life of my own as well.

Confused, tired, I tried, but failed, to close my mind to what it would mean – the treatment. Apparently non-invasive. Electric pulses through the brain? That sounds invasive to me. Someone so small, unable to make her own decisions – huge, life and personality-changing. She is my daughter. It's my job to protect her but also make her life better, fuller. Can I justify doing it? To her. But can I justify not doing it? For me.

I have been told, given assurances, that she would be less anxious, free from repetition, made 'more normal'. So, I tell myself she would be happier but, in truth, is it to wipe out the parts of her that make my life unbearable at times, most of the time?

Her consultant says that repetitive behaviours are part of her 'condition', her autism; the subject of obsessions might change over time but obsessions will always be there and she won't be able to alter the pattern she chooses each time. There is no medical treatment here, just acceptance and strategies, supposedly to help us both.

I feel trapped in a life of monotony, predictability and repetition, never my comfort blanket. I feel I am spiralling further and further down into depression and loneliness. Don't I deserve a chance to be happy?

I pulled on my dressing gown and put on my slippers. I shuffled downstairs, my tired eyes flitting anxiously to the doormat, feeling sure I saw a flicker of white, like glimpsing a dark movement out of the corner of the eye, scanning for spiders, but there's nothing there. For now. I was breathless, scared of what might come.

I made a cup of tea and wondered fleetingly if tea tastes as good in California where the clinic is, where Neil is, Rosie's father. My stomach churned.

As I did every single day, I took the cellophane-wrapped tray out of the cupboard and, slowly, heavily ripped open the wrapping and carefully placed twelve beige cupcakes on a pink tray. Not randomly, no, but as I always do – in three rows and four columns. I describe it as such in my head, my accountancy days far behind me, but seeing it appearing as a spreadsheet pleases me. I took the ready-made white icing. I carefully squeezed the required amount onto each cake and robotically smoothed each blob of white icing across the top of each beige cake.

I suddenly thought back to that awful day months ago when the inexplicable happened. That day, THERE WAS NO ICING SUGAR. I remembered not believing what I was *not* seeing; the heat creeping up and having to sit down shakily on the kitchen chair, taking deep breaths. There was no way Rosie was going to cope without carrying out this current, long-running obsession.

I had thought through the options to cope with this disaster:

1. Fake my own death – maybe a bit overboard;

2. Run away – getting nearer;

3. Be the first forty-eight year-old woman to do the two-minute mile in a dressing gown and slippers; locate and pay for ready-made icing from the twenty-four hour Asda and get back in another outstanding slipper-footed two-minute mile.

Okay, fake my own death.

Racing against time, my brain kept revolving like those funfair rides that make you feel nauseous and spin you back to the same places, time after time. Then, in a stroke of genius I had remembered the white Polyfilla which I'd used to patch up the result of some other crime I'd committed, probably having bought Asda's own brand Wheat Biscuits, instead of Weetabix themselves. If I could get the consistency right, I'd thought, I could pass it off as icing. And ta-dah, I had. It had smelt a bit weird, but she'd had a cold, thank God. Disaster averted.

I was attempting to shake off the memories of Polyfilla day when, as always, at 7.33 a.m. Rosie appeared, my five year-old beautiful bully. As I observed her messed up dark wavy hair, her sleepy chestnut eyes, my chest tightened. I wanted to help her, to free her, to rid her of the compulsions, but shame and fear fought for air, pushing down love and acceptance, buried much deeper within me. Or maybe not existing.

I avoided looking her in the eyes, but Rosie never

looks people in the eyes anyway. 'Good morning, mummy.' That's as good as it gets. No hugs, no kisses.

This morning, as with every morning, she sat at the kitchen table, pink tray with twelve beige and icing-ed fairy cakes in front of her. Jelly tots in two pink bowls, six red jelly tots in one and six green jelly tots in the other. Without fail, she places the red jelly tot on the white icing on fairy cake A1, then green on A2, red on A3 and green on A4. I hope every day that she will put green on B1 but it's always red and then so on until green on C4.

I was distracted by the hem of her pyjama bottoms, now far too short for her, but I can't find exactly the same "My Little Pony" pyjamas in her size. She is tall and long-limbed, as I am, and this set is not going to last much longer. I wondered if I could get the pyjamas in time to wear in the clinic in California for her treatment. If she goes to the clinic. My head tightened, forcing me to sit down, nauseous and clammy.

After eating her daily breakfast of beige, dry Weetabix, Rosie prepared herself for school. She prefers to get herself ready. She doesn't dress weirdly, as if she's been blinded half-way through the process, as Daniel, her brother, did when he was that age, left in charge of his own dressing destiny: odd socks, T-shirts two sizes too small and a migraine-inducing colour combo.

I heard Rosie giggling, Daniel singing badly on

purpose as he brushed her hair. I swallowed a sob. I used to feel happy although confused at their closeness, surprised by Rosie's laughter and emotion.

Now I feel confused by decisions that I need to make. Neil, her wealthy but absent father, is desperate to show his love by paying for treatment to change Rosie into something unknown. Daniel, who loves and lives with Rosie, is desperate to protect her and keep her the same. And what about me? I think I am desperate to do both, but really I want life to be easier for me, however that comes.

Apart from Neil, Daniel is the only person who can make Rosie laugh and brush her hair; two skills alien to me. Daniel, pseudo parent, seventeen year-old brother. I grimly, and not necessarily jokingly, think she will have to have a crew cut when Daniel goes to university in six months' time.

I forced myself back to when it all began, the cake thing, not the being Rosie thing – that came before she entered the world. Helpfully, mother, who calls Rosie 'funny little thing', which could be sweet but isn't, told me one day that if I hadn't shagged Neil, the American, I wouldn't be pregnant – wow, you couldn't get anything past her – and that if I hadn't gone back to work when Rosie was six weeks old then she wouldn't be 'well, like she is'. Helpful.

I'd had to give up work anyway; the nurseries couldn't cope with Rosie. I'd tried a few. Mother wouldn't have her, because that would interfere with her tennis and her lunches. Dad would have loved to have her but he doesn't make the decisions. Never has.

I went back to that fateful day, the day of her third birthday when I thought in some desperate way that icing cakes together would bring some bonding to our rather odd relationship. Of course, Rosie wouldn't eat the icing-ed, jelly tot-ed cakes because they were no longer beige. That's how I got round the Polyfilla incident. Also why I'm not size eight anymore but size eleven and three quarters. Although now I only have two a day, one for breakfast dessert – it's a real thing – and one for lunch dessert.

My accountancy mind started working out the amount of cakes Rosie had put jelly tots on. I had bought trays of twelve beige fairy cakes, ready-made icing and jelly tots every day since two days after her third birthday. Two years, fifteen days.

Day 'aged three years plus one day' was the worst to date. Not even Daniel was able to console Rosie over something we couldn't understand: screams, tears (mainly mine), things being thrown, me being punched, Daniel crying, until an exhausted and red-rimmed-eyed, snot-running Rosie tipped the contents of the kitchen bin over the floor, found an empty packet of jelly tots, took the pink tray out of the cupboard and mimed putting jelly tots on the cakes. All I could do was nod as tears streamed down my face.

Daniel, white-faced with exhaustion from the futile attempts to calm us both, slumped with me on the kitchen floor. I tearfully promised Rosie she could decorate cakes before the special needs group the next day.

Gulping back tears and air, shuddering with every breath, she came over, sat on my outstretched legs and laid her head on Daniel's lap and, after a few more jolting breaths, fell asleep. Daniel and I, like conjoined twins, heads together, felt the wracking sobs of each other's bodies until we too fell into uncomfortable sleep.

Back in my beige life I calculated the amount of trays of cakes I had bought – two years of trays was 730 trays, plus fifteen days was 745. 745 recyclable trays made into pens or something; 745 'not yet recyclable' cellophane wrappers thrown into the kitchen waste along with a binload of guilt; lots of icing – couldn't work it out; 745 multiplied by 12 cakes – 8940 cakes, so 4470 each of red and green jelly tots.

They don't sell just red or just green jelly tots, and I had lost count of the amount of bags I'd bought. I once tried a different brand of jelly tots which, to my untrained eye, looked the same as Rowntrees in their pink bowls. I never did again.

Ben, Kayleigh's son from the special needs group, lines up dinosaurs in size order, or was it alphabetically now that he knew their dinosaur names? I couldn't remember. It would be a lot cheaper. It wouldn't involve me. That selfishness rearing its head again.

I knew why I was calculating. Something I've always done, blocking everything out, trying not to think of the white envelope landing on the doormat. The envelope with its foreign American stamp and strangely spelt words in a letter offering details of a treatment that could change everything.

As regular as clockwork, Rosie came downstairs at 8.10 a.m., her hair in a complicated French plait. I'm sure Daniel watches YouTube for inspiration, or he's destined to be the next Nicky Clarke!

The doorbell rang ten minutes later and Rosie happily switched off the TV, the same programme I had watched with her more times than fairy cakes decorated. I opened the door, with relief, to Saint Lorraine who whipped Rosie off in a flurry of patient exuberance. Saint Lorraine takes Rosie to school, twenty-six weeks of term so far, minus one – the first week.

Saint Lorraine had been witness to the car crash of me taking Rosie to school for that first, excruciating, week. The tears, the screaming (mine) and the tears and screaming, punching and biting (Rosie's) were put down, by the school, to Rosie not wanting to be parted from her mother, and vice versa.

But the truth is that it wasn't the reason, it was

that Rosie hates new things. She wasn't keen on Miss 'sing-song-y' Hall, the Year 0 teacher who tried prising Rosie off my legs the first two days. Then it was the turn of Mrs 'slightly exasperated even though it was the beginning of term' Bennett, the Head of Early Years, who managed a day. Next came Mrs 'frighteningly fearsome but apt to give up easily' Watkins, Office Manager, for Day 4, and then, on Day 5, finally and successfully, it was Mr 'the name fits perfectly' Good, the Special Needs Coordinator.

Saint Lorraine, until that point only known as the childminder from Number 46, had stayed that last fifth day while I composed myself in the reception area waiting for 'The Perfect Mothers' to disappear from the school gates before I dared to cross the dreaded school playground. I didn't mind 'The Other Mums', who were as dishevelled and wary of 'The Perfect Mothers' as I was, not catching the eye of any Perfect Mother.

'The Other Mums', the mums with the quirky, different children, like Rosie, were more my type. I felt a knot of shame that I was teetering on the edge of moving back towards The Perfect Mothers, leaving The Other Mums behind where I didn't think I really belonged.

That day Lorraine led me exhausted and dazed back to her house. The house was vibrant, full of colours: orange, yellow and red, no beige required here. Spicy Caribbean food and cups of sweet hot tea were put in front of me; no cakes, I noticed with relief.

Smells of Jamaica flooded my senses, strange and foreign noises as Lorraine's hair click-clacked with beads as she moved around; music playing loudly in the background, people talking and shouting as if arguing but erupting with laughter. Hugs and kisses and emotions bounced off the colourful walls, warmth coming from every pore of the house.

I used the excuse of the morning's events to explain the tears of happiness and longing that spilled out in that alien house. Lorraine offered to take Rosie to school for me.

Thank you now-recently-canonised-in-my-mind Saint Lorraine. I couldn't bring myself to tell her, someone so motherly and kind, to explain what might lie ahead; I couldn't say those words in this happy, bright house; to feel judgement on my decision. Or was it keeping the arrangement that meant more to me?

All of a sudden I realise I'm slumped in a kitchen chair – an hour passed since Rosie left. Tears falling onto paper, staring straight ahead, unseeing. The letter had landed, white, on the doormat, the decision, black and white. Appointment times on weirdly swapped month and day format; explanations; words jumping out – "magnetic", "pulses", "electric", "transcranial".

My mind fills with the whirring of Neil's pleading, Daniel's fury, mother's indifference, Rosie's beautiful face swimming in and out of focus.

And then I notice. Something I hadn't seen this morning, worrying about pyjamas. Something they said couldn't happen. A green jelly tot on fairy cake B1.

CLEMENT JEWITT – who am I?

Who indeed! Few of us humans really know the answer to this question, which might take many lives to come to terms with. I identify seven previous lives, (so far).

In this life, I was born in London during the Blitz, an experience which left permanent scars, but hey!, what doesn't kill you makes you stronger.

Now, in my eightieth year. I have been through three different careers, and nearly embarked on a fourth. I have been married three times – the first two wives died. Four children have their own families.

With a fundamentally introvertive character, (type five for Enneagram aficionados), I have read extensively, and have always written about what I am concerned with or am doing. Numerous essays resulted, a little fiction, and some poetry. Publication occurred from time to time. The little story in this volume I concocted in 1986 to amuse a few librarian acquaintances: it needed editing!

EXPERIENCES DURING LOCKDOWN

Coronavirus. The best way to see this is as a wake-up call, for we are in the middle of a global collapse. I recall the 1957 and 1968 viral epidemics. I was in London, and hardly noticed the epidemics, which, by the way, were as severe as the current one. We, the population, were treated as self-reliant and capable of sensible decisions – therefore no shutdowns.

In recent decades governments have introduced successive protective measures to look after citizens in various needful ways. All well and good, very laudable, but the corollary balancing outcome is that we have become sheep, children, governmentally treated as unable to be sensibly self-reliant – so Lockdown. There is a lot of fear about.

Stay at home if over seventy! No way, not me thank you! Near forty years of refusing annual 'flu vaccines have left me with a strong immune system. I had a very mild bout of Covid-19 in early April, lasting a few days. My existing immune system dealt with it. A recent test showed that the antibodies had gone. The requirement to face the virus effectively leads to adopting a positive attitude: I tell myself, 'I refuse to bow to this dead thing!'

Facing that fear when out dog walking or shopping, causes difficulties in emotional life. I found I was growing increasingly angered. To overcome that needed care.

Nowadays I try to view those fearful people with compassion which seems to be part of the energy we need to get through this interlude.

VISIT TO A LIBRARY
Clement Jewitt

This fragment, in an unknown tongue, on an unidentifiable paper-like medium which resists analysis, fell out of a large piece of Chinese coal when it was broken with a hammer. It has recently been deciphered and rendered into more understandable contemporary English by Clement Jewitt.

... my terra-nano library, skin grafted on at birth, as was my right, I lost with my leg in the accident. In my job, which I was reared to, one must have the facts at his leg side. Accidents are so rare nowadays, it was going to take some time to sur-create my new library leg. Accordingly, I decided to find and hopefully make use of an old static library.

I vocalised this thought for Henry, (I'm a bit of an antiquarian – I enjoy making speech sounds), who coughed, whirred, clicked and spoke, 'The nearest one is Europe West, in a space called Paris. It is not known whether it is intact. It has probably not been visited for one thousand years. That is all I have, Mr Bossman, Sahib, Sir.'

He amuses me, Henry: there appears to have been possible crossed programming on his Culture Complex, maybe because of leakage from others adjacent in his birth factory. I did think of having it cleaned, about a century ago, when I acquired him, but I grew to like the idiosyncrasies. He's full of old information bits. I think he may have been a librarian, when there were such things; before my time.

I drifted into my INTACT (Instant Negative Time Actual Contact Terminal) and "Formed" my historian neighbour with the control under my left arm, skin grafted on at birth, as was my right. After a pause, his presence filled my space and me as the walls faded and swirled.

'I wish you'd use the Advance Warning,' his "voice" vibrated in my head. 'I was outside pruning my four dimensional roses. See, I've still got radioactive dirt on my gloves.'

I didn't look. I don't use the Visual, can't bear to see people. Instead I "said", for the millionth time, 'When will you live in the present instead of pretending to grow things which don't exist?' And before he could return his stock reply to this, I continued, 'Do you know anything about the old static libraries? My new leg will be a few weeks and I can't wait that long.'

'Ah, thought I'd hear from you soon about that. Always knew you for an impetuous youth.' (Silly old fool! Just because he's a hundred and forty years older than me, he thinks he can claim eldership.) 'I got that thought,' he "said", without commenting further. 'Where were we? Oh. I've already consulted the records, but there's not much. I'll fetch my notes.'

No fetching needed now, but the old phrases linger. I must connect with a semanticist about that one day.

'Right. There was one library for each area, typically underground, datamation was stored bio-magnetically, on primitive structures. I think they were called machines then. Not known whether they still function. That's about all I can connect you with, except there was usually some kind of enquiry analysis probe. I'm quoting from an old text here: I'm not sure what it means. You'll have to physically go and find out, I think.'

I thanked him for his help, and Unformed his presence.

I was afraid of that, I thought. I had not been outside for seventeen summers, when I last thought I detected life out there. Very few people go out now.

Speculatively, I fingered the toggle on my forehead, skin grafted on at birth, as was my right, but decided that with my leg so recently lost, my metabolism might not stand the strain of Immediate Matter Transference. Besides, I had no idea where this Paris was. I would have to go in person, physically. But how?

Henry would know.

'Henry,' I spoke.

He appeared through the wall: 'I am at your service, Mr Bossman, Sahib, Sir.'

I explained my dilemma.

'Oh, that's easy, Mr Bossman, Sahib, Sir. We have an early Travelporter vehicle. I keep it in good order in case you should want to go sightseeing. Also, I myself know the location of Europe West Library near Paris, for I formerly worked there. I shall see that the vehicle is informed of these requirements and otherwise made ready immediately, Mr Bossman, Sahib, Sir.'

So he *had* been a librarian. A pity he had been partially rebuilt as a House Hold: he might have been useful on this Travel.

Riding North over the derelict landscape in the Travelporter, an old machine with windows, I passed the time re-enervating my ocular nerves, which had long been passed into suspension as redundant. This was a tiring experiment, since the use of the eye involves the co-ordination of fleshy muscles, which were weak from disuse. Besides, this blasted, dying world is not good to look at. Henry's "sightseeing" is a word mostly forgotten these days. But he was built long ago ...

Pulling shut and sealing my Envelope, I left the Travelporter and approached the strange unfamiliar building. Henry's instructions to the machine were accurate, as they should be. There was a shape, which resembled a door, and over it was the remnant of a sign, proclaiming "Area Libraxxx 291, Europ West, Paris", which was partially obscured by frost. I wondered how far south the ice was now.

Speculating on the amount of energy I would require to pass through the shut door, I noticed a word on it – "Approche" – and other words obliterated. I decided to follow the instruction, since nothing could harm me. As I did so, the door slid to one side. This was encouraging. It must have a kind of Admit mechanism. I didn't know they were that old. That it still worked heightened the possibility that the library might be of some use to me. I was without thought at this point assuming that updating had continued ...

Inside were two curious paths leading downwards, formed of a succession of horizontals and verticals. They were what could only be called linked tracks, undoubtedly meant to move, but extremely crude in design and materials. With difficulty, for they were awkwardly designed to impede rather than facilitate movement, I made my way down one of them, musing on the imperfections of the people who had needed strange odd paths to transfer from one horizontal to another.

At the bottom was a wide expanse of further doors, side by side. I approached the nearest and it, too, opened before me. Better and better, I thought.

I found myself in a very large space indeed, and wondered again at the inadequacies of these ancient peoples. We have no need of such vast spaces. The effect of it was rather uncomfortable. On each side were rows of what must have been perceiving machines, fronted by crude seats. It reminded me of an ancient Ambience-only entertainment I had once seen.

My entry must have activated the place, for those machines began to hum and flicker and, from the end opposite me, something began to move. I quickly detected that it was a machine, but how quaint. It moved actually in contact with the ground, on a set of small revolving discs. When it came near, it spoke, in a somewhat artificial voice, with archaic words, 'Welcome to the Library, Sir. I am the Librarian. May I take your hat and coat?'

Nothing surprises me, naturally, and nothing can harm me but, nonetheless, not knowing what was meant by 'hat' and 'coat', I energised my Armour, skin grafted on at birth, as was my right, and replied coldly, 'What I have is mine.'

'As you wish, Sir. We are glad to see you. We shall now be able to improve our statistics.'

He was not a threat, then, so I de-Armoured and remarked, 'The place still seems operational. When was it last used?'

'To be precise, Sir, four thousand and twenty-seven years, four months, sixteen days, five hours, forty two minutes and seven seconds ago, counting to your entry, Sir. The last visitors stayed a long time, and none of them finished their searches. In the end, I had the Janitors clean away the remains. What was your query, Sir?'

I was about to reply when I became aware of an

acute tingling in my head. It was most uncomfortable, though vaguely familiar. As I paused, the Librarian said, impersonally but kindly, and with a touch of pride, 'Nothing to worry about, Sir, that's our Query Probe, which I have just switched on. It assesses and quantifies the concepts in your head which you are struggling to express through the inadequate medium of language. I perceive that it is a little irritating in its present form. However, there are improved models on the way, Sir. Or, perhaps there were.'

So that was it. The same principle as our familiar INTACT, though vastly less refined. It must surely be part of their pre-history.

I was beginning to savour this excursion into the apparently living past, so, ignoring the laughable simplicity of his programming, I told him to switch off his Query Probe and tell me more about his library.

He dutifully acquiesced and explained, at length, the chain of mechanism that led from the Query Probe to the Information Selectors which could range, as he put it, 'in mere nanoseconds' over the few billion billion items of information in the store. He showed me the Rapid Reproducers which could bring to the inquirer within seconds anything from a single item to complete texts, either to be read or heard on the screen or taken away in tangible form. He had evidently been programmed to show pride in it but, to me, how cumbersome and slow it was.

Why, I had an equivalent amount of quanta-electrons, for a different purpose, under my right thumbnail, grafted on at birth, as was my right.

I spent forty hours there, vainly searching for the information I required. Francos, as I named the Librarian, was puzzled and solicitous, but no help whatever. The Query Probe, even after I had reformed it to a more efficient design, was no help either. I had gained some information about that culture, however, which would please my historian neighbour. Apparently the Librarians were designed principally to act as foils to irrational tendencies in the people of that time – further evidence of their immaturity.

I concluded, reluctantly, that these old libraries were not self-updating, as are our modern personal libraries, which meant that the resources there were as out of date as the mechanisation. My Travel, therefore, was largely wasted, apart from the somewhat tiresome pleasure of experiencing something of the life of our ancestors.

I further concluded that there must be what might be described as a control centre, where fresh material would have arrived and redundant material ejected.

I explained this to Francos, who replied that he did not know the meaning of what I said, but that there was a place within the Library to which he was forbidden access, as a Librarian, where I might find what I sought, and that he would direct me to the place, as I seemed to be a Master.

I decided to examine this before I left. Following Francos' instructions, I found myself in a long tunnel, barely large enough to accommodate my bulk. I detected a door at the end, and a broadening out of space beyond that.

There were signs of structural problems in the tunnel, cracks and dislocations, increasing towards the door. The door at first did not open, but a quick pointing of Power changed that. On the other side of the door was a gargantuan ...

[The script breaks off at this point. There is no date, signature, or other mark of identification.]

TARIA KARILLION grew up in a tiny cottage in the grounds of a Welsh castle, and is supposedly descended from an infamous pirate (much to the amusement of her fencing coach at the time). But despite her historical background, after an accident with a flight of stairs, a copy of "The Hitchhiker's Guide to the Galaxy" and a nasty attack of gravity, she became hopelessly addicted to science-fiction, particularly climate related themes and the future of AI (although this particular story is notable for containing neither).

A Literature Degree, a journalism course and some gratuitous vocabulary overuse later, Taria's stories appear in a Hagrid-sized handful of anthologies and literary journals, and have won enough Awards to fill his other hand. Despite this, she has no need – as yet – for larger millinery.

Forthcoming plans include a volume of her collected works and the formula for calorie-free chocolate. Not much to ask for, really.

EXPERIENCES DURING LOCKDOWN

The global pandemic and ensuing Lockdown has been, for Taria, similar to other dramatic events in life, a time for reassessing one's perspective. The extended removal of our normal freedoms has illuminated that upon which we should perhaps be focusing more – or less.

The tragically massive loss of life, the ongoing risk

with which we all now live, and the phenomenal, daily acts of bravery of front-line workers has renewed our appreciation of our fellow beings.

Let us hope and pray that this bigger, nobler perspective – the best of humanity – endures.

It is ironic that, in a time of non-contact, the words of Aung San Suu Kyi (the first and incumbent State Counsellor of Myanmar and Nobel Peace Prize Laureate who lived under house arrest for twenty years for pioneering democracy) were never truer: 'We will surely get to our destination if we join hands.'

SCIENCE, LOVE AND GUANO
Taria Karillion

The bicycle was in its usual place. Not that the word "usual" was actually applicable to the top of the campus flagpole. Verle Coby squinted up at it through the October drizzle, before muttering to himself and plodding back across the quadrangle, slippers squelching on the lawn.

None of the other staff or students gave the bike a second glance. Odd occurrences at the university were two-a-penny and either dismissed as pranks or ignored altogether as Somebody Else's Problem. The competing smells of the science block welcomed him back indoors and Coby took the stairs two at a time.

Back in the lab, he huffed as he tossed his wet slippers into a corner with a colony of fast food boxes and paper coffee cups.

'Y'know, you really ought to throw that lot, matey, before a rodent hotel opens a franchise in it. S'bad for your weight too ... *and* our noses.'

The muffled voice called from behind a tall rack of scientific equipment. Muffled through what sounded like lunch. Coby arched an eyebrow.

'Lab Partner – *not* mother! Anyway, show me *one* photo of you *not* eating! So, where's YOUR middle-age spread, that's what I want to know!' He sighed, glancing down at his own.

The chewing and slurping continued.

'Well, my friend, if you spent less time hiding away in here and actually socialised a little, at the gym with me, maybe you'd lose that excess! AND did you know Frantastic Fran from Organics goes to the gym? She looks even better in Lycra. C'mon, you anti-social bugger! Why do I keep asking! Would it be so bad to have a few friends in your life?'

Coby reached for his iPod.

'Drowning you out with Stravinsky now?' He took a deep breath in as his ears filled with a swell from the string section. Phil was right, though – Fran would look great in a binbag, not that Coby ever noticed what people wore, unless it was a lack of safety goggles.

The clock chimed the hour and he found himself at the window without remembering getting up. Sure enough, crossing the quad with those long legs and usual sunny smile, there she was ... Francesca.

A tapping on the glass startled him. More so when he realised he was doing it himself. Fran turned at the sound and beamed up at him, waving. Coby's hand ignored the paralysis affecting the rest of his body and waved back. How long had it been since he had this feeling? Not since ...

'Open the window and invite her for LUNCH, you fool!' shouted the food-garbled voice through an orchestral crescendo that felt as if it was as much in Coby's ribcage as in his ears.

Too late. Fran was already scurrying away.

Atop the flagpole, with its still-dangling metal "flag", wheels turning slowly in the breeze, a seagull landed and decorated the saddle with a splash of white. Coby rolled his eyes. Why hadn't he chosen something else to trial his teleporter on?!

'I hate that bike.'

As he removed his headphones, a loud belch erupted from behind the racks.

'I realise why you hate it, pally. Shall I tell you? It's because it symbolises your diminished status since the divorce. Sorry to be blunt, mate. BUT, as it happens, Fran doesn't care much about status. What she *does* enjoy is physics and classical music *and* the same nerdy sci-fi shows as you, and you'd know way more about her if you actually *spoke* to the woman!'

Coby shook his head and started tapping at his keyboard, frowning intently at the screen.

'Thank you Phil O'Sophical. But supermodel looks *and* a Nobelled late husband? With ME? Not a hope.'

A shrill tinging sound was audible from the quad. Through the leaded window, a seagull was tapping at the bicycle bell as insistently as an impatient customer. Coby returned to his chair and typed: *Attempt 67 – same lateral displacement as before. Target missed.*

Was that the smell of egg sandwiches? Coby was about to pass comment on it when a far-back falsetto voice sailed across the room.

'Hellooo, I'm Verle Coby – I'll never measure up – I've o-o-only invented teleportation and play five instruments AND have a full head of hair that waves in the wind like a boyband wannabe, and ... ' Hoarse laughter gave way to choking sounds and colourful expletives, followed by a heavy thud.

'Phil? Phil! You all right?' Coby asked, looking up.

'Ach, don't rent out my room yet, laddie. I'm not going anywhere. I'm as much a part of the bachelor furniture as this stuff!'

Verle tapped a gauge and shrugged.

'Well ... um ... women go for bald guys too, y'know, Phil ... apparently ... too much, in my ex's case. Anyway, heads up. Goggles on. I'm bringing it back. Incoming in three, two, one!'

Whirring and whining grew in volume from a cable-fringed dais across the room. With a clanging clatter, the bike reappeared in a shimmering, dazzling flash, followed by a squawking thud at the window as the seagull hit the glass and slid down the pane. Coby frowned at it, opening his mouth and pointing, before sitting down and scribbling at speed.

Another hour chime and an unscheduled nap later, Coby woke with an almighty sneeze. Gazing at the glinting motes swirling in the air, he noticed something in the dusty surface of the bench. Words! He squinted and pushed his glasses back up his nose.

'Is this you, leaving messages for me in the dust, Phil?' he tutted.

VERLE – TO DO: Eat proper meals, see friends, stop wallowing, and do the DUSTING!

Coby raised his eyebrows and rubbed his eyes.

'Going for the subtle approach, eh, Phil? Phil! Are you there?'

It was too quiet, until there was a *rat-a-tat-tat* from behind him. Coby roused himself.

'Did you leave your keys behind again?' he called.

'I'd be thrilled to have some in the first place, actually!' replied a soft voice.

A woman!

Coby straightened his dishevelled clothes and scrambled for the door, wishing he knew the whereabouts of his comb. The panelled oak creaked open with a sound that mirrored his surprise.

'Fran! I ... it's ... um ... nice to see you! I ... er ... ' His brain fumbled for something to say that wasn't 'Wow'.

'Hello you! I've not seen you in the dining hall for a couple of weeks and ... well, I thought I'd check you were okay. May I come in?' She smiled.

Oh, that smile. That infectious joyful smile that made October feel like June, and those ethereal, green eyes, hypnotically large behind delicately-framed glasses, and the ever-present, out-of-place wisp of hair across her brow that he was desperate to stroke back, and not because of OCD.

159

After a moment longer than was comfortable, Coby realised he was staring, and wafted an arm at the room.

'Of course, yes, please do! Um, sorry about the mess. The cleaners aren't allowed in at the moment, in case they ... disturb all the ... stuff.'

Fran glanced around, taking in the state of the room – the piles and the papers and the bin, overflowing with lord-knows-what and topped with a frosting of bright yellow tape. She frowned.

'Wow, has this not been emptied since the ... '

She closed her mouth and smiled.

'Why don't you let *me* help you tidy up a bit? Maybe you could make some tea?'

'Sure. And thank you. So kind.' Coby pressed his palms together, fingertips to nose, with a momentary smile.

Fran beamed and twirled into action as Coby rummaged for mugs and spoons and jars, more than half-watching her as, with graceful sweeps of her arms, she transformed the lounge area and Coby's side of the lab, swiftly transforming the post-burglary-like disarray into a state of order and neatness that even his own mother couldn't have found fault with. The fast-food container mountain rapidly disappeared into black plastic bags in a similar series of captivating, waltzing manoeuvres. She was clearly quite the dancer.

After a few more minutes of companionable silence, Fran tied a burgeoning bin bag, swinging it

160

into place outside the door and sinking onto the sagging little sofa under the window. She smiled as Coby brought over a tray of mugs and Jammy Dodgers.

'Sorry about the kiddy biscuits,' he blushed, sitting beside her and passing her a *Star Wars* mug. 'They're Phil's, but he won't mind. Especially as I've made him a brew. He'll probably be back any minute.'

Right on cue, there was a reverberating belch and a tinkle of glassware.

'Talk of the devil! You snuck in quietly, mate! There's tea over here!'

Fran rested her hand on Coby's and gazed at him with those puppy eyes.

'Listen, Verle. I like you. A lot. And I *don't* believe any of the gossip, but you have to accept the truth about Phil.'

Coby frowned.

'What do you mean?'

Fran's voice was as soft as a bedtime murmur. As soft as the touch of her fingers over his hand.

'Verle ... Phil hasn't been here for weeks.'

'But he's right over th...'

'Verle, listen. What happened ... it *wasn't* your fault. The poor guy choked, right in front of you. It must have been *awful*. But you have to stop blaming yourself. It's messing with your head, hon.'

'She's right, y'know.' Phil's voice sounded as if it was coming from the bottom of a well. 'You're a decent guy. You tried to help, but hey, at least I went with my favourite food in my hand! Now, get a grip and move the hell on, okay?'

'Verle? Verle! Focus!' Fran's eyes pooled a little, but the warmth of her smile was no less radiant. 'We *all* talk to ourselves sometimes. Some days it's the only way I can get a sensible answer! But this? Well, let me get you some help. Please?'

She sneezed and turned, reaching to struggle with the curly, gothic window latch.

'You *really* need some fresh air. How about we take a walk? Down to the river?'

Verle felt a glimmer of something. Hope, maybe? Like headlights in fog, memories faded in and out of his mind's eye as his stomach gave a lurch. How could he have blanked it all out? And why?

'Verle?' Fran was patting his hand and looking around.

'Perhaps you could ... you could even clean up that antique bike and we could take a ride together?' She rose and picked up a cloth. 'Here, let me wipe that bird muck off the saddle for you.'

'NO!' Verle sprang out of his seat. 'Um, I'm sorry, I mean, *please don't!*'

'I don't mind. Honestly. I grew up on a farm!'

'No, you don't understand. That's ORGANIC MATTER! And the saddle was *clean* before it went!'

Coby's eyed widened as he crossed the room in three quick strides. 'My machine has only ever worked on *inorganic* test samples. This is a HUGE breakthrough! HUGE! I ... I have to make notes! I want a pen! Where's my pen?' He patted his pockets, looking around.

Fran reached out and rested her hand on his shoulder.

'What can be so important that it can't wait an hour or two? Wouldn't you like a proper meal?'

Verle chewed his lip, then exhaled long and hard before taking Fran's hand and squeezing it.

'With you? Very, *very* much. But first, I just need two minutes!'

He twiddled knobs, pulled levers, turned himself and Fran away from the bike, and waited for the flash. Picking up the binoculars, he peered out at the flagpole. An odd sensation crept over his face – he could feel himself smiling.

The bicycle was in its usual place, still with its splatted saddle.

But right now, Verle Coby had something more important to focus on.

163

ALAN JOSEPH KENNEDY, originally from Glasgow, Scotland, has been living in Spain for the past twenty-seven years. His first degree was in musical composition and he has worked as musical director for theatre, English teacher, gravedigger, sales rep and recently (the last fifteen years) as a storyteller, travelling round the country for nine months of the year.

He started writing five years ago whilst training as a creative coach and found that most of his clients were struggling writers. Inventing stories has since become his main creative outlet. At the moment, he is halfway through an MA in Creative Writing at the Open University.

Apart from the creative arts, Alan's other passions include yoga, snorkelling, cooking, and learning languages. He has one daughter, and he is currently studying Basque, his partner's mother tongue.

EXPERIENCES DURING LOCKDOWN

The pandemic struck Spain while Alan was working in the Basque country, one thousand miles from home.

On Thursday, March 12th, he was performing in a school near the French border. That evening, he received several emails from various clients cancelling his work for the following week, due to the schools closing. Of course, he knew about the virus which had been affecting Italy and had recently arrived in Spain but, like everyone else, he thought it would be a passing news item.

Alan was fortunate to be based in his partner's house while working in the North of the country, so he decided to prolong his stay. However, on the Monday, he and his partner could only leave the house to buy food as the government had declared a state of emergency and the whole country was on strict Lockdown.

One by one, his clients for the rest of March through to June pulled out and he was left with no work, no income, and miles from home.

Although the Spanish government, like every other country, was unprepared for the pandemic, self-employed people, including Alan, were given a small monthly income to tide them over. His normal lifestyle of being on the road nine months of the year, never having time to relax, and giving performances every day, ground to a halt, as did his hope of finishing his Master's next year.

Still, he and his partner signed up for a daily online yoga class. He put himself to write two or more hours a day, a habit with which he is incredibly pleased. He took out ten story seeds which he had generated over the past three years and tried to give them form and body. Alan has since moved to San Sebastian permanently and retired from work. Maybe, if the situation improves, he will resume his acting activities but, if not, he will surely enjoy his new life as a pensioner.

UP MEMORY LANE
Alan Joseph Kennedy

Up an alley called Memory, months after it crumbles down, years after they raze the Lane, a decade after the recollection seeps away, the murdered residents still sigh, still grieve. Echoes of those colourful inhabitants of a vaguely remembered cul-de-sac bleed through time, giving future generations a legacy not to forget, not to forgive.

Eight o'clock on BBC Radio Four.
Seven days till Christmas on this Arctic Tuesday morning.
Today's phone-in tackles the controversial
Motorway to Nowhere and the tenants with nowhere to go.

As always, Jake Cartwright from Number 9, alert as a sparrow, game for a giggle, tries to beguile his neighbour, Minerva Washington.

'All right, my luvver? A lush day for strollin', a perfect mornin' for a jaunt. Won't you stretch out your legs with me?'

Minerva wraps a scarlet woollen scarf tighter round her face. 'Do cease badgering me, or it'll be a five-year stint at her Majesty's Pleasure you'll be heading for. My limbs are of a superb length, thank you all the same. I'll be keeping them well away from you, stretched, folded or otherwise.' She tosses her leather satchel over her shoulder, turning aside for a moment to take a sly puff on her inhaler.

'Come on. Just the once. For old time's sake.' Jake adjusts the straps on the battered tenor saxophone case in which he carries his unfinished prosthetic leg.

'No sake, old or new, no motive young or ancient could possibly entice me to walk out with you.' The half-smile in Minerva's eyes wrestles with the muffled coolness of her voice.

'We can stay in, if you're so inclined. Ah, f...!' The sax strap grazes his nipple ring. Jake winces and clamps his crutches to his ribs. Not cool to fall over. 'Sinead will be here any minute now.'

'Heavens to Betsy! Straight up? It's too bleeding chilly to continue this chit-chat. If you'd only carry on with whatever you layabouts do. Let me fly rather than have that interfering plumber wreck my morning before the day has properly dawned.'

Minerva scans the dimly lit road, spots the hunched up hooded man in the park. 'Isn't that Sinead's ex?'

'Ain't he got a restrainin' order hangin' over his loaf?'

On an ice-covered bench under the oak, Bexley Lynch scrawls in his "Anger Management" notebook, binoculars at his side, pencil ripping the page. His chapped hands shiver as the fierce December frost stiffens his fingerless mittens.

Tuesday, bloody Tuesday! Back in the old street. Who'd have thought it, eh? Look at them. Peg Leg chatting up the Dancing Duchess. Creeping Jesus slinking out from his burrow. Twats! The lot of them. Nothing changes. Yet! Young Bex will soon fix that.

On the bitterest morning of the winter, Rhys Summer slithers out from the frozen, moss-encrusted basement of Number 3 with his habitual Grateful Dead T-shirt, purple shorts and sandals. Head first, then neck, tortoise-like.

A specialist magpie, he doesn't hoard clothes. Out-of-date newspapers, bits of magazines, receipts from the supermarket, scraps of his Muses are his obsession of choice.

On the floor round his mattress, a poster for Minerva's new masterpiece, Sinead's shopping list of plumbing appliances; Doctor Pinky's love letters lie in the form of a cross.

Ten crumpled pages with names for his unwritten novel peek out from a ripped back pocket: Court of Strangers, Alley Cat Alley, Up Memory Lane, Road with a View. After six weeks, he is no further on than the title.

As he fingers his late mother's wedding ring on his pinkie like a Rosary, his cracked lips move without a sound. Rhys peers into the newly purchased owner-occupied house.

In her recently painted kitchen, Doctor Pinky Bhali kisses the fading photo of herself and another white-coated woman with "Love you forever, Ghouri", written in lipstick.

She pins the Polaroid between tonight's Street Party invitation and a picture of sunny children swimming in a bomb crater. With the thought of Ghouri's cancer-wracked body fresh in her mind, it's too painful to return to the refugee camps.

Pinky sneezes for the fifth time since waking up. She looks under the sofa again. Where has she put it?

Eight thirty news from BBC Radio Four.
The mayor guarantees swift action to prevent
rebellious tenants blocking progress.
The mercury will stay below zero all month.
Today's weatherwoman ...

Like a badly written soap opera, Minerva and Jake's fruitless banter brings forth a barren yield. Twice a day, her 'Yes' dangles from mango balm solaced lips, aching to be picked. Jake, big talker with breezy finesse, body swerves the hint.

'No, then? You won't mull it over, dreckly? I'm the dog's – I mean, a proper catch.'

Jake rehashes the tired script which used to work – before that lorry trashed his bicycle.

Minerva checks out Jake's leg and the space where the other one should be. She does like him. He's

169

funny, makes her laugh, but – no, she couldn't, possibly.

'Watch out! Here comes the plumber. All right, Sinead?'

Soon, the pair are chaperoned by Sinead O'Rhea and her son, Dick, from the last house. The mother is six foot two, frizzy red hair and muscle bound. Her son, short, with a body like puff pastry, risen without a mould. Even by Memory Lane's catholic standards, a strange family. The gable end side window gives them an aura of glamour.

Sinead, in her work overalls, eyes them up and down.

'As I live and breathe! If it's not our favourite couple. How are we all cuttin' today? Lookin' grand, Minnie. As do you, Jake. As per usual.'

Minerva raises one eyebrow, Jake smirks, Dick gapes.

Intoning repeatedly, mantra-style, Sinead continues revising gas leak procedures with her son. 'First, check for withering plants, then watch the animals. The dogs sense it in advance of anyone.'

Dick nods. Drawing out a piece of scrawled-on paper, he mouths the words: 'Moist jute in the joints freezes, causing a chink when it thaws.' A mouthful to memorise. His stepfather, Bexley, wrote it down for him, before turning coat and blagging a job with the council.

📻 *The nine o'clock news on Radio Four.*
Debate on the new motorway is underway.
Experts estimate rehousing
could begin next month.

After his tenth cigarette, Bexley Lynch continues scribbling. His "Bailiff Department" embossed bag, full of undelivered eviction notices, lies on the ground beside a transistor.

I'll tell her to her face. A proper earful she'll get. Me, Tattooed Lady's old man, chucking her out. Just the job! New motorway. Progress! Bags first go on the sledgehammer. Best served iced. Sinead, the damn plumber, rabbiting on with the squatters, her dimwit son too (not mine, thank God). At least MY feet are on the ground.

'How's business, Sinead? Plumbin' away? Bringin' Eve's ale, takin' Adam's excrement. Do you earn supplements for sewer jobs? Time and a turd? Flushed with that money you're earnin'?' A joker by birth, Jake brightens the atmosphere.

Minerva blanches. 'Excuse me, my breakfast is not fully digested.'

Sinead snarls at the dancer. 'Digest the image of four foxes, spotted out our lateral lunette, polishing off your cat. Fair put it away.'

'Heavens to Betsy! My Blossom died a year and a half ago! Get a life! You loathsome, meddlesome, foul-mouthed, scandalmongering busybody. I'll shove the leftover cat food down your fat tattooed

171

throat.'

'Talking of foxes,' Jake interrupts, 'look! Bexley the Missin' Lynch! Judas workin' with the enemy! D'you hear the latest eviction news?'

In his stench-soaked midden, Rhys Summer never reads daily papers; he goes to the shops once every two weeks, picking up thrown away veg at the Monday market. Being Tuesday, he stashes his food hoard for the week, stuffed into his health hazard of a fridge. Today is the day Summer rummages in the trash bins

'We'll work through the doctor's, won't we, mam?' He licks the ring.

Across the road, Pinky combs her flat from top to bottom. No luck. She showers with her usual ginger lemon gel, "guaranteed to put zing" into her morning. It never does. Not with that pathetic trickle of lukewarm water. She searches for Sinead's number on the party invite.

Good afternoon on this freezing day and welcome to BBC Radio Four.
Today we are looking at three safe ways to check for gas leaks.
Tune in at two thirty.

Back from lunch, Bexley is in full tilt. A broken pencil points at his feet. Pulling his council anorak hood down over his ears, he stoops to caress a short metal handle sticking out of his holdall.

Let's see who's useless when she's homeless! No more street parties. Not for her or her kinky mates. Houses falling like skittles these days. Hers is next. Strike and out!

On Memory Lane, our four streetmates collide ... as magnets, constantly changing poles, attracting yet repelling.

Sinead whispers. Dick grins. 'Leave it out, ma. A one-legged carpenter? Did he make his own wooden leg?' Dick guffaws. Jake strokes his sax case.

Exhausted after the morning's rehearsal, Minerva doesn't join in the jesting. 'I'm dying for a nap. Far away from Sinead's gormless, gutless parody of an offspring.'

'Hey! Watch it! Mother says I have plenty of guts, lots of gorm.'

'Hark at him! Bye. Off to my woodwork class. Catch you later.' Jake winks, waiting for a signal.

Minerva looks away, patting her inhaler in her pocket. 'You'll have to race to snare me, if that's your gist,' she wheezes.

Sinead runs her tongue along her lips. 'You can catch me ... not as swift as I used to be.'

'I'd rather catch the 'flu. Is it true you've got a penis tattoo coming out of your lady parts? Is that why you called your son Dick?'

Minerva snorts. Sinead giggles, pulling up her jumper. 'It's a spanner. Dick's real dad inked it.

Roughly drawn, I know. He loved the drink, he did. Bexley wanted me to get rid of it. Chucked the pig out instead. If you show up at the party, you can explore the whole – toolbox. Good craic. Don't invite the creep. He'll jot down everything I say.'

Rhys Summer has found a photograph in the rubbish. He peers at the blurred colour image of ripped tents, a woman's smudged face and adds it to his "altar". He has a retentive brain, a writer's mind. No books – yet. The title eludes him. Once that comes …

He files the clutter carefully in his mind. 'Must keep tidy, mustn't we, mam?' Externalising his inner chaos, Father Pritchard told him. A branch cracked outside his window. It's her in the photograph.

The doctor, head to the ground, retraces her steps of the previous night, scrutinising the pavement. Nothing. Clenching her teeth, she pulls out another nicotine chewing gum from her back pocket. Pinky looks over at the hooded figure hiding behind a shrub in the park.

Bexley's tongue darts between his cracked lips; sweat drips from his pallid brow, freezing like pearls on his anorak. Five o'clock. He fondles the pencil, steadying himself against the oak.

By any means, fair or foul, the Mayor said. I've got a surprise for Sinead. Do I give a monkey's? Not bloody likely. My revenge's chilling by the moment.

Under the only working street lamp, the four come into each other's orbit one more time, shivering against the icy wind. Jake eyes up the dancer's Afghan coat. 'Expect I'll see you in the flesh at the orgy or in the beef in my dreams, Minerva.'

'Not if I see you first.'

That's two appearances she won't be making. Not tonight. The after-show cocktails come first.

Sinead wipes her greasy hands on her overalls, takes a deep breath. She hankers for Jake to "dream of me". She claps her palm over her mouth, then spits out a mouthful of tallow.

'If you hear a scream comin' from my gaff, that'll be me dreamin' of you.'

Minerva grabs her bag. 'Must dash. Two hours to go till the dress rehearsal. You coming to the show tonight, Jake?'

Sinead smiles. 'Don't miss the Housing Co-op second anniversary party at Number 13.' She pins a badge, "No Motor No Way", onto his jacket, tweaking his nipple ring with her pinkie. Jake gasps then returns her wink.

Minerva knifes Sinead with a withering look. She swallows twice. She'd let him. Maybe. Maybe! Why can't she tell him?

'Party! Ballet! Mmmm. Tough choice.'

Sinead sticks two fingers in her mouth. 'All talk, no action, Mr Jakelin Cartwright. Must crack on

myself. Fixing the wee Scottish doctor's shower.
Wonder if she'll slum it enough to thank me.'

Good morning from the BBC on this,
the coldest Christmas Week this century.
Later, last night's crucial motorway vote ...

Doctor Bhali yawns as she glances at her watch.
7:00. Shit. Can't spend another day hunting for it.
No work until the afternoon shift. After a bout of
sneezing, Pinky blows her nose, then a kiss at
Ghouri's photo. She rubs her thigh muscles, aching
from dancing all night. 'Glad I went, Ghouri. Felt
part of the street. Bed tempts. Hey! Who's rifling
through the rubbish? Hoy you. I told you before.
Beat it!'

There's a thought – it just might be there. No, I
couldn't. Have to soak my hands overnight in
bleach.

As he empties his pickings onto the table, Rhys is
half in a dream. A night owl, he isn't usually up or
out at that time, but the uncommon smell of gas
kept him from sleeping. He mumbles a prayer at
the Muses' shrine beside his mattress.

Bexley glowers up at one of the windows,
stroking the metal handle seven times in rhythm to
the church bells with building excitement.

Sorted! Trusty old hacksaw, a nick in the pipe. Fire
Brigade will blame the Banshee! A quick kiss or two from

the wrecking ball. Out by Friday, extra five hundred quid in hand, lovely jubbly!

A still inebriated Dick O'Rhea weaves along to Number 7. What had his mother said about leaks? Where was she?

'Use washing up liquid on the joints', or was it jointing lotion on the wash? No bubble, no flow. Do NOT strike matches. As if I ...

Illuminated naked shapes in Jake's bedroom window interrupt Dick's musings; his hand shoots down his trousers. 'Minerva, Minerva, Miner..!'

Just then, the dancer snakes along the street carrying a corsage of red roses. Dick squints again at the window scene. When the two passionate silhouettes gyrate around, his mother's unmistakable tattoo comes into focus. Too late! Wiping a sticky palm on his toolbag, Dick O'Rhea scuttles away, tripping over the bottle of Fairy from the bag.

Minerva scoops it up – spots the steamy pageant unfolding – reaches for her inhaler – it's not there – then passes out on the icy pavement, legs splayed.

Out in the street nothing stirs. The ice makes indoors the best choice. The other frost-covered windows are opaque, except Rhys's. A greasy finger has rubbed a peephole through which his blue eyes sneak a look. Dick! Nothing else to see ...

Hang on. Something moves under the wilting shrub outside his neighbour's house.

177

A fox!

The shrill yelping startles a hung-over Pinky into peeping out her window. A fox! With Ghouri, she saw one in the desert. She grabs her camera, inching the door open so as not to scare it. The animal scratches at something on the ground under the dying bush, sniffs then vanishes. Pinky gasps.

A lighter.

The gold lighter Ghouri left in her Will. At last! As she pulls a cigarette from her purse and puts it in her mouth, a lone tear gleams through her glasses.

Looking around, Pinky Bhali grins at the to-ing and fro-ing of the spanner tattoo scouring the frost off Jake's window. She has discovered a home, at last.

Someone darts out from the basement across the street. Pinky's martial-arts-honed reflexes kick in.

Rhys eyes Pinky tiptoeing out. The fox sniffs then flees. Nose twitching, Rhys kisses his ring and shoots out. As he tosses himself through the air, he half hears Dick shaking a box of matches in the next house. As she swerves the lunge, Pinky glimpses a scarlet scarf – Minerva is sprawled beside it.

When Bexley picks up his bag, after throwing the redundant eviction papers into the bin, he catches a whiff of the gas. As he strides off to dial 999, he pats an imaginary wad of cash. A deafening blast spins him around. A sawn-off length of pipe bayonets his gaping mouth, nails him to the oak. His half-filled notebook opens under his twitching feet.

 We interrupt this programme to update you on the South London gas explosion headlines.
Scottish doctor saves lives. Five deaths confirmed along with the dream of a young dancer.

Down the Lane called Memory, the blast wipes out most of the street. Weeks after the buildings come down, the final houses still standing are bulldozed.

Months after they raze the Lane, the council shelves the scandal-ridden "Motorway to Nowhere".

A decade later, echoes of those deaths, the now-famous choreographer's lost limb, cries of the former colourful occupants of a vaguely remembered yet memorable cul-de-sac, scream through time, never forgetting, never forgiving.

❀ ❀ ❀

DAVID MCVEY lectures in Communication and Literature at New College Lanarkshire. He has published over one hundred and twenty short stories and a great deal of non-fiction, from academic papers to a column in a football programme.

David enjoys hillwalking, visiting historic sites, reading, watching telly, and supporting his home-town football team, Kirkintilloch Rob Roy FC.

EXPERIENCES DURING LOCKDOWN

David believes that Lockdown has had its moments. 'If I missed going to the theatre, to football, to galleries and museums, at least my wife and I were working at home. And, unlike some, apparently, thrown together by Covid-19, we get on well for protracted periods.

As for many, reading was one thing that helped me through, though since I had no bus journeys to and from work, I probably read less in total than I would have in normal circumstances.

Writing was also therapeutic; if I couldn't talk to colleagues and students, I could make my characters talk to each other.

Animals helped – cats (we have two) are a sort of National Health Service with fur. Also, my wife has a part-thoroughbred mare that we had to visit every day, though without going through the stables (Lockdown!).

For the first two months of Lockdown, we walked a kilometre every day through woods and fields and over two little hills to the horse's enclosure and during the ensuing weeks we watched spring burst into growth.

Of course, it hardly rained during late March and April. Lockdown would have been a different experience if it had.'

SKELP
David McVey

Light drives out silence.

It was just after seven o'clock. Outside, dogs barked in a throaty chorus, babies bawled and mothers screamed at children. It was a weekday in March, but Jessica had the day off.

She switched on the kitchen transistor radio and flinched as raucous pop music erupted from it; her cleaning woman must have moved it to that new Radio 1 station. She twiddled the dial until a sweet string section sang from the speaker ("Radio 3" it is called now), then she chopped fresh fruit – apples, pears, mandarins – into a bowl and poured the last of the Greek yoghurt over it. She'd have to pop into the delicatessen for more today.

She ate her breakfast, alternately sipping from a glass of orange juice – that was running low, too. An early bus rumbled past outside, which gave her the idea of taking the bus into the town centre and leaving the car in the garage. It would only cost about a shilling return and perhaps she might meet some of her neighbours, talk to them, even get to *know* them.

There was a bus at half-past nine, so at twenty-past she pulled on a short coat over her trouser suit and grabbed a scarf before walking down the driveway beneath trees dripping with cold tears.

The house was a solid structure in grey stone with

two bay windows like bulging eyes. The driveway extended out to the main road, opposite the street which led into the big council scheme, Marmion Avenue.

She crossed the road to the stop. Three women were standing there, waiting for the bus to arrive. One of them was carrying a baby in a kind of nylon sleeping bag.

'Hello,' Jessica said. She recognised two of the women, including the one with the baby.

All three nodded, and one of them went as far as to return a shy 'Hello,' but then they turned back to each other and to their interrupted conversation. Their talk came in rapid, staccato bursts, in a strong West of Scotland accent that Jessica couldn't follow.

From behind came a deep, bronchial roar, reminding her of the lions on one of those David Attenborough documentaries, Jessica later thought, but at the time she and the other women leapt with fright. They swung round and saw, in the garden behind the bus stop, a small, scrawny boy, wearing filthy school shorts and an untucked blue school shirt. He made another deep sounding roar, laughed, gave a gap-toothed grin, and ran off through the garden.

'See if I get my hands on that wee nyaff ... '

'It's a good hard skelp he needs.'

'He'll get one aff me if I ever catch him.'

'Who is he?' asked Jessica.

There was an awkward pause before the woman with the baby said, 'He's Tam, Doris and Erchie McKenzie's boy. He's no the full shilling but he's still supposed to be at school instead of making an erse of himself.'

'And running through other folks' gardens as well!'

The women resumed their conversation. Jessica was isolated again, but the bus arrived minutes later. It was fairly full. While the other three lit cigarettes and climbed upstairs, she ended up on the long seat behind the driver, facing backwards, wedged between a fat man reading a racing paper and a smartly-dressed middle-aged woman.

Jessica pulled out her *Guardian* and began to read the front page. She needed to make the effort, given the difficulties involved in having it delivered.

The local newsagent had pulled a face. 'Not much call for *that* paper here,' he'd complained.

She had reached the end of the first page, and was wondering how to turn the pages on such a crowded bus when she heard a voice asking, 'Excuse me – do you live in the old manse?'

It was the woman on her left. She smiled, saying, 'Yes, I do; how did you know?'

'Oh, it's fairly obvious. I'm Annie Gordon. I used to live there.'

'Ah. So ... '

' ... I'm the minister's wife, yes.'

There was silence for a few seconds. Then Annie

continued, adopting a confidential tone, 'We weren't happy living in such a big house when everyone round about lives with so much less. There are a couple of old miners' rows in Waverley Crescent, at the other end of Marmion Avenue, and we persuaded the Kirk Session to sell the old manse and buy one of the miners' houses. Angus calls it "Incarnational Mission" or something of the sort.' Jessica seemed a little bemused, and Annie asked, 'And what made you move here?'

'Well, my partner, Simon, he's a lecturer at London University but he's got a job at Glasgow University, starting in September. I'm in marketing, so I started looking for a job in Glasgow and I managed to get one right away and had to move up first ... '

'But why here? The old manse, with a big council scheme across the road and another beyond your back garden. I thought you Londoners could afford to buy houses anywhere?'

'Simon was keen that we live close to ordinary people. We're both socialists, you see. The house is ideal because it gives us plenty of room for ourselves and the twins but it's right in the heart of the community. And we chose Braeturk because long ago my family lived here. My great-grandfather moved to London when he was a young man.'

'Twins?'

'Yes, Gerald and Thomas. They're nine, at boarding school in the Cotswolds.'

They rose together as the bus approached the main town centre stop, standing on the open platform as feathers of smoke curled down from upstairs.

As they parted, Annie said, 'We must meet up for a coffee some time.'

Jessica smiled and nodded, without enthusiasm.

After the library and the bookshop and the stationer's, she went to Roger's Delicatessen.

'Aye, fresh in this morning, the Greek yoghurt.' Roger, big and bearded, spoke in an unmistakeable Home Counties accent, but with the odd 'aye' and 'wee' thrown in.

'If you didn't stock it, I'd have to go into Glasgow for it.'

'And for anything that wasn't fish fingers or baked beans or tinned peas.'

Jessica grinned. 'Oh, and I need fresh orange juice.'

Jessica arrived at the homeward bus stop carrying a large brown paper bag packed with items from the delicatessen. ('Plastic carrier bags will never catch on,' Roger had said.) There was no sign of Annie.

The bus was packed this time and she was forced to sit in the smoky dankness upstairs; it was as if she was in a Victorian opium den which shook and rattled.

There was a rush down to the platform before Jessica's stop but she was near the rear and was able to hop onto the pavement as soon as the bus came to a halt.

The street was busy with teenagers heading back to the local secondary school after lunch. She walked behind two older girls who suddenly stopped as a small, dirty figure jumped out in front of them.

'Gonnae let me look up yer skirts so's I can see yer knickers?' shouted Tam McKenzie and burst into laughter.

Two women, fresh off the bus, emerged from behind Jessica and stormed up to the boy before he could run off. One grabbed him while the other struck him sharply across the face and shouted, 'It's about time ye learned tae behave yersel, ye wee shite!'

Tam's watery sniff might have been partly a sob as he ran off down the street.

'Aye, he's been asking for a skelp like that for a long time,' declared a man who'd been on the bus, his words drawing murmurs and nods of approval.

Jessica simply acted on instinct. She faced the two women and said, 'I don't think that'll help. Using violence, *hitting* the poor child ... '

The women regarded her with amused contempt. One of them replied, 'Ye're no in Buckingham Palace now, hen.'

'Buckingh ... I live *here*. I'm on ... '

She'd been going to say 'I'm on your side!' but the two women had gone, laughing, on their way, and

187

the larger group of people was dispersing. Even the two schoolgirls looked at Jessica with sly humour. Tam had disappeared.

Later, Jessica sat at her desk, idly doodling on the blotter, trying to think of ideas for the TV campaign she was managing for a company which sold Venetian blinds; so much for her day off.

The phone rang. It was Annie.

'Hello, Jessica? I wonder if you'd ... '

'Annie, hello. Sorry, but how did you get our number?'

'It used to be ours, remember? I felt a bit odd dialling it.'

'Oh. Of course.'

'Look, the Easter Garden Party is coming up. It's not as grand as it sounds. It's held in the church grounds and there's tea and baking and games and things for the children. It's the first Saturday of the school holidays.'

'But we're not religious.'

'Oh, don't worry about that. Lots of people come. It's the free food. I thought it might give you a chance to meet people, make new friends.' There was a pause, before Annie added, 'I sense that you need friends.'

Jessica, suppressing a sob, reluctantly agreed to go.

A week prior to the garden party, Simon phoned. After a brief chat, he announced that he'd booked a skiing holiday in Austria for himself and the children. 'I know you can't get the holidays so early in your new job, so this gets us out from underneath your feet, doesn't it?'

'Is that it, Simon? Is that all? You're abandoning me here.'

'Don't be dramatic, Jessica, I'm just ...'

'It's because *you* got a job in Scotland, because *you* wanted to move here, that I *am* here, on my own, isolated.'

'Jessica, I'm disappointed. You're really being very selfish.'

Simon had changed. *They* had changed, and there was something else, unsaid, unshared, that Jessica instinctively knew he was withholding.

She rose late on the day of the garden party. It had been a difficult week at work, and she felt she might lose her mind if she ever had to consider again the benefits that Venetian blinds brought to modern lifestyles.

She dressed smartly in a tweedy skirt suit, the nearest she had to the kind of outfit she associated with the religious, and set out on foot for Braeturk Parish Church. There were lots of people about, in their gardens and on the pavements, but while some turned to look at her, no one spoke.

She was halfway along Marmion Avenue when she came to a narrow driveway between two houses. The church was at the end of this drive, set among some bare, scruffy green lawns and a small gravel car park. The church was a low, concrete affair, today surrounded with stalls and marquees. There was a roped-off area where children played organised games. Annie was in there, roughly dividing the children into two teams.

'Jessica!' she cried. She detached herself from the children, leaving them in the charge of two burly teenage lads and a thin, greying man her own age – her husband, the minister, presumably.

Jessica smiled despite herself. It was unseasonably warm and the tweed skirt itched and irritated. 'Well,' she said, 'I'm here!'

'Glad you could come. Let's introduce you to some people.'

'I'm not taking you away from anything, am I?'

'Oh, no. Angus can cope, and he has a couple of boys from the youth fellowship helping too.'

Annie showed Jessica into the largest of the marquees where Jessica smelt hot tea and coffee and warm baking. Cakes and pastries and small pies were piled on a central table with a large tablecloth, the tea and coffee being served from urns.

People who already had their tea and food sat on plastic stacking chairs round circular tables. A loud murmur of talk surrounded the two women as they made their way to the food. Annie introduced Jessica to people at the tables they passed, but she knew she'd never remember any of the names. Faces swam before her, unrecognised, unrecognising, as if in a bad dream.

She noticed that most of the women her age were comfortably dressed in slacks or jeans, with a few fashionably turned out in mini-dresses. Small children darted about the marquee, risking a shower of hot tea as they nearly capsized passing adults. Jessica thought briefly of Gerald and Thomas, of a sun-warmed piste and colourful skiwear, then tried not to.

At the central table, a jolly fat woman in an apron – Annie announced her name, but Jessica instantly forgot it – poured her a cup of tea and pressed her to collect some baking on a paper plate. They sat at a table where Annie introduced her to the two other women there – Linda and Shona. Linda had a small boy on her lap, aged perhaps two.

'Have you any weans, Jessica?' Linda asked.

'Weans?'

'You know – children.'

'Oh, yes. Gerald and Thomas, twin boys, nine.'

'And where are they now?' A hint of accusation crept into Shona's enquiry.

'Well, they're at a boarding school in Gloucestershire.'

'Oooh!' exclaimed Linda and laughed. 'Boarding school! Fancy that!' Then she affected to address her child. 'Now, don't you be getting any expensive ideas, Ian!' Shona laughed too.

Jessica tried to smile.

'Will they be coming up for the Easter holidays?'

asked Annie.

'No.' Jessica was slow to respond. 'Their father is taking them on a skiing holiday.'

'Och, you poor thing!' exclaimed Linda. 'I didnae know you and yer man were separated.'

'We're not.' Jessica had to fight back the tears as she rose from the table and ran out into the spring sunlight.

She stopped in a quiet spot to catch her breath, and saw Annie's husband and the two boys playing games with the children which involved a huge circle of brightly-coloured parachute silk. There was lots of running and a constant tinkling of children's laughter as the parachute was shaken into enormous rainbow waves. On the open patches of grass, pairs and groups of adults chatted and laughed and joked. A few of them paused to glance at her, briefly, and then continued talking.

The voices and the laughter, the colour and the movement, blurred and merged, became alien. She had never felt so far from home.

A small figure darted up to her. A child. She hoped it would not speak.

'Can I look up yer skirt and see yer knickers?' laughed Tam McKenzie.

Jessica thought of Gerald and Thomas and Simon and the gulf that had emerged between them and of everything she was losing, everything she had already lost, and a rage consumed her, causing her to raise her right arm and bring it down sharply on

Tam's jaw. He shrieked and ran off, though he was already laughing by the time he saw a couple of older girls he was keen to annoy.

'Well done, hen,' came a woman's voice. 'That's what the wee shite needs.'

'Mind yer language!' said her friend, 'We're in the church, here!'

Jessica fled home, drew the curtains, and sat quietly at her desk, waiting for darkness to arrive.

For hours she sat there, while outside the buses growled and dogs barked and children shouted. Several times the phone rang – Annie, probably – but she remained motionless.

Eventually darkness fell and with it an unstill silence.

MICHAEL MORELL lives in Melbourne, Australia. He is a writer and a teacher and enjoys how they are rarely mutually exclusive of each other. What he appreciates best about both is the sense of hope they bring for how things are going to turn out.

Some of the places and experiences that have coloured Michael's lived and written world include projecting 3D films at London's IMAX, bisecting Australia's red desert in a Kombi, furnishing fancy folks' homes in fabric, and getting hitched in pre-marriage-equality Taipei.

He is currently kneading into shape a YA novel inspired by his adventures working in an ice-cream kiosk on Brighton Beach.

EXPERIENCES DURING LOCKDOWN

During Lockdown # 1, Michael eventually came to appreciate the benefits of life inside – comfort dressing and eating, moving at a slower, self-determined pace, and having spare time to write, solve Sudoku, master TikTok challenges, or just sitting and staring.

Regardless, when Lockdown # 2 was announced, he deflated. That's Melbourne's vibe at the moment. Flat. This time round, the feeling of "we're all in this together" seems to have dissipated.

Michael has been focusing his energy on engaging

with his students. It's one of his favourite parts of the experience. It forces him to get inventive and puts his writing skills to good use. It could never replace seeing their faces in front of him, though, rather than through a screen. He tries to be led by their example; being present and finding joy in smaller, more immediate adventures. 'Imagine how you're going to remember this,' he tells them, insinuating this is merely a temporary inconvenience until we get back to how it used to be. But, for them, every day is a new normal.

180 DEGREES
Michael Morell

The sameness was transforming him into an automaton. He had performed the morning walk to the station so often, it had become an unconscious act. It wasn't until he was standing on the platform, staring blindly at the tracks, that he became aware.

Clouds had moved across the morning sun, their shadow jolting him out of his stupor.

He looked about the platform, which was quickly filling with fellow commuters, and wondered how he had gotten there. He realised he had no memory of the walk, nor of leaving the house, dressing, showering, or even of having breakfast. It would have been muesli, because he always had muesli. The morning ritual was unchanging and automatic.

He had a regular spot on the platform, between the bench seat and the rotating advertising. Being down the end of the station and toward the front of the train meant less competition for a seat.

By positioning himself between two stationary objects there was less chance of others entering his personal space. Everyone had their own ways of shutting out the world; folded arms, headphones, a newspaper, a scrolling thumb or finger. The space inevitably filled, one commuter at a time. Each claimed their temporary territory at a distance suitably equidistant from the next, as in a huge elevator; all facing forward, together but separate.

The sun reappeared from behind the clouds. He resumed his meditative stare, enjoying the returned warmth on his face. He sensed movement in his periphery. A leaf fluttered from a tree, gently chartering a haphazard path through the air into his field of vision. It landed squarely on the steely tracks where he had been staring, and balanced itself rebelliously. Still.

The approach of the train was anticipated collectively. Those around him started to shift; phones pocketed, bags lifted, feet shuffling forward. Statues coming to life.

Moments later, the announcement came, redundant, "Arriving on Platform Two, the 8.16 train to Flinders Street Station". Reluctantly, he pulled himself out of his numb bubble and joined the shuffle toward the yellow line. Clumps began forming at the spots where the train's doors were expected to open; a giant game of roulette.

When the train arrived, those in the clump readjusted, attempting to retain pole position, always with an appropriate balance of force and civility. The carriage was mostly full. A couple of lucky roulette winners might squeeze into a spare seat, thigh to thigh with the passenger next to them, knees knocking the passenger opposite and avoiding eye contact with everyone.

He found himself on the outer fringe of the door clump. The doors pulled open and stony faces peered out, resentful of the imminent intrusion, as if they had been sucked into the inertia, as dirty bath water does when it gurgles down a drain.

He shifted his attention from the backs of heads down to feet. His gaze slipped into the shadowy gap between the train and the platform edge. It seemed cool and quiet down there. Peaceful. Impulsively, he stopped moving.

His feet land squarely on the yellow line.

The last few passengers squeeze into the carriage. He looks up, taking in the sight of the packed carriage before him. His feet remain still. He turns his head and casts his eyes down the platform. It is empty.

The signal for doors closing beeps, yet his feet stay planted. He faces the train. Amongst the jumble of bodies wedged together inside the carriage, his eyes meet a lone face staring back out at him, the expression asking, "Well, are you getting in, or not?" His body responds by way of an answer. His feet lift, stepping back slightly, as if picked up by a breeze. He pivots away from the train and begins walking back down the platform.

He hears the doors slide shut behind him, sealing his decision with a gentle thud. He marches faster, with more purpose. The train starts moving, in the opposite direction. Both pick up speed. Two objects in motion, as if unified by an equal, yet opposing, force. Carriages start to blur as they rush past, the last one whipping by at the precise moment he reaches the platform exit.

The red lights of the level crossing begin to flash, and the warning siren clangs, spurring him on. He picks up pace again, jogging now, down the exit ramp to the road running perpendicular, and slips through the closing gate.

A second train approaches, heading in the opposite direction. It pulls in to Platform One as he skips across the tracks. He pushes through the side gate and up the path to the station entrance. He weaves his way through the departing passengers and hurtles across the platform, into the first set of open doors. The warning signal beeps. The doors slide shut, as they had a few minutes before, but on a different train, a different platform and a different destination.

He collapses into a vacant seat and rests his head against the window as he catches his breath. He looks across at the empty platform opposite. It's as if no one had ever been there.

His eyes lower and rest on the steely tracks below. Only minutes had passed since he had been staring in a mindless trance at the same tracks, but from a different perspective, flipped 180 degrees. Who knows where he's heading?

He recalls the trajectory of the leaf and its decisive touchdown. His eyes remain on the tracks as the train moves, but his mind is still on the leaf. He wonders where it is now.

MELANIE ROUSSEL grew up in Berkhamsted, Hertfordshire. It's a quaint and quiet little market town which has its few little oddities, such as a castle which isn't really there and a totem pole overlooking the Grand Union Canal.

She then moved to North London, which is neither quaint nor quiet. She works in television production as a Junior Production Manager. It's often a hectic job so any free time she gets goes into writing.

Melanie is a member of the London Writers' Café and runs a speculative fiction blog at Melanie Roussel Fiction. She is currently working on a science fiction story while also submitting a speculative fiction/hard-boiled detective novel to agents. She has been published in the Henshaw Three anthology with her story "Rock 'n' Revolution" and has also been published in "Scribble Magazine" as well as the "10 Minute Novelists" site.

EXPERIENCES DURING LOCKDOWN

Melanie's natural habitat when writing has always been in cafés and libraries. She is inspired by people-watching, catching snapshots of their lives. So, when Lockdown hit, it was a blow to her creativity.

It took a while to find her motivation again. Long walks in woods, gardens and commons replaced her London scene and they have become a different pool of inspiration.

Lockdown has also given Melanie time to focus on her craft. She has been applying for competitions and taking classes.

All in all, while she says she can't claim any great uptick in her word count, she feels as though she has had a chance to think about her writing in a new way.

AFTER THE CREDITS ROLL
Melanie Roussel

I awoke in the cold green light of dawn and experienced, for only the second time in my life, that blissful morning amnesia. I wasn't sure where I was, or what I had to do today, but I was ready to slip back into unconsciousness.

The mood shattered as I felt something move beside me. My hand darted out reflectively for my Glock, lying on the ground beside the mattress. I tensed. The thing gave a grunting snort.

Oh. Yeah.

I groaned internally, letting my grip loosen on the gun as I screwed up my eyes. I tried to cringe myself out of existence. Shit.

Blissful morning amnesia well and truly obliterated, I rose carefully from the mattress. I glanced back briefly, considering waking him up; dealing with the situation as the adult my mother, (not to mention my Squadron Boss), hoped I was. A train of thought which lasted a generous five seconds.

I crept away, searching the room for my uniform and boots, locating them in the rubble around us. I moved to the door as quietly as I could, avoiding the broken glass. The stairs creaked like hell's rusty gate. But when nothing stirred upstairs and I made it out onto the street, I breathed a sigh of relief.

Outside, the once suburban road was eerily silent.

No revving of car engines, no shouts of children or barking dogs. Before the war, that fact alone might have been alarming. But the world was finally free of the blood chilling clicking and buzzing sounds which had come to haunt everyone's nightmares. Today, an icy silence sounded like victory.

My lips curved as I saw the number of alien carcasses in the street vastly outnumbered our own. That wouldn't be true in the long run, of course. Not with the damage I'd witnessed in Paris and Oslo. But seeing these eyeless, tentacled fucks rotting did wonders for this girl's tired soul. Some had a mucky green foam oozing from, what I'd been reliably assured, mouths. They looked like mangled, fanged waste disposals.

'Laura?'

Aw nuts. I forced a friendlier smile. Toby had managed to pull on his trousers and shoes. No socks, though, and an unbuttoned shirt. He was out of breath, but anyone who spends two-thirds of their life in a lab usually were. Oddly attractive though, in that made-for-black-and-white-photography way. The jawbone, the eyes, the wild hair. It struck me again how different he was from the classic beefcakes I was normally attracted to.

'Were you ... '

'No!' I interrupted, a little faster than I'd planned. 'No, I wanted to see it for myself. Armstong's Neurotoxin actually worked.'

The sky above was shimmering with that hazy

green, caused by the neurotoxin we'd released into the atmosphere last night. Harmless to humanity, though the nerds believed it would destroy a third of the bird population. A small price to watch these Lovecraftian abominations die choking on their own frothing lungs. Horrible way to go. Painful too, I hope. A lesson to anything else out there that wanted to invade the Earth. Yes, we're prepared to poison our own sky to get you fucks off our planet.

Toby took in the sight of the dead aliens with clinical, scientific interest. 'Professor Armstrong is a genius,' he declared. 'She's been going at it non-stop, ever since we captured those test subjects in Portugal. She'll get the Nobel for this.'

'Chemistry or World Peace?'

He stepped forward, his hand reaching out. I pretended not to notice as I checked the safety on my gun. I laughed a little, that forced smile still in place. 'Don't sell yourself short, remember. Without your last-minute breakthrough, we'd never have made it this far. Armstrong is singing your praises. After all, they chose you to be the lead scientist on the deployment team.'

'I couldn't have done it without you. When that thing grabbed my leg – if you hadn't been there, I'd be dead, for sure.'

'Just doing my job,' I replied. Again, a little too quickly. God, pull it together.

'So,' he glanced around. The silence of a hundred dead aliens filled the space. They seemed to delight in my awkwardness. 'What do we do now?'

I felt the full-body cringe return. As cheerfully as I could, I remarked, 'Well, I have to report in. Get into the air. It's ninety minutes to Marham. You should get back to Armstrong. She'll be having a field day with the alien tech.'

'Sure. But I meant ... and then?'

'And then, what?' Why did he have to do this?

'I mean ... last night. The sky turned green, ships crashing out of the sky.'

'It was all very Michael Bay.'

'You – We kissed.'

'Caught up in the moment.' It sounded lame, even to my ears. He took another step forward, clearly gearing up for it. 'Laura, these last three months working with you ... the world has been upside down for so long. Aliens attacking. Actual aliens! Half of Europe on fire, scrambling to catch up with a massive technological gap. The human race uniting in a way no one ever thought possible.' He took a breath. 'When we first met at the base, I thought you were some stupid macho grunt.'

'And you were some asthmatic, wimpy egghead.'

'But I was so wrong.'

God help me. Crash landing on that mothership and fighting my way back to Earth with nothing but my Glock; flashlight and a knife had been easier than this.

'Toby,' I saw his shoulders slump. Guess he's more perceptive than I'd given him credit for. 'I trust you with my life. Hell, I trust you like the guys I've trained with, lived with, survived wars with. That makes you my friend for life.'

'But a friend?'

'What do you know about me? Actually *know* about me? What do I know about you? Only that you're able to reel off the periodic table by heart. And you know how an alien's respiration system works. But not if you leave the toilet seat up or like the Sex Pistols.'

'I don't like the Sex Pistols.'

'There, you see? It would never work.'

'Even after we had ... ?'

It was a shock to realise I'd slept with a man who couldn't even say the word 'sex' without blushing. Did scientists not have locker rooms? Wonderful! Now I feel bad, on top of bloody awkward.

'It was fun. But not life changing. I mean, it was great. You were great.' I waved my hands around, trying to grasp the point which to me was bloody obvious but to which he was oblivious. 'Toby, we'd just survived goddamn Armageddon! The whole situation was ... emotionally charged. Besides, thanks to you, we know how to kill these things. They're going to send me to Paris with the toxin, and,' I paused, collecting myself, 'what did you think was going to happen?'

'But I thought ... all this has to change your perspective on things.'

'Does it?'

'Obviously it does! It changes your priorities. It has to. I don't want to spend my whole life alone in a lab. What about a family?'

'Woah, Toby, I ... '

'No! Not at the moment. Think about it. For the first time, we understand what it means to be part of this universe. And, apparently, not a friendly one. We have to consider what makes us human.'

'Do we?'

'Yes!'

I thought about it for a moment. The man was a genius. I'd realised that from the moment I'd met him. One of Britain's most talented scientists. So I guess big thoughts were his right. But even though London was finally free, there were hundreds of cities around the world still under siege. I was itching to get back into the cockpit of my Lightning II.

Cautiously, I said, 'I get that technology is going to change. New satellites and weapons and stuff. I don't see how that matters to me.' I shrugged. 'Do you really think that one apocalypse makes a difference?'

His hands were in his pockets. I watched as he absently kicked one of the gangling black and red tentacles out of his way.

'Toby, you're the hero of the hour. Nobel Prize? Scientific papers? You're going to be famous! Think of all the interviews the press are going to want with the brave egghead who left the lab, wading into an alien stronghold to arm the giant diffuser?'

'The atmospheric dispersal unit.'

'Whatever.'

He was buttoning his shirt, pushing his fringe back out of his face. Thank fuck. I had no idea what I would have done if he had gotten teary. 'Maybe they'll put my photo up at the Cambridge Science Park. Or at least publish my papers.'

'See? Plenty to look forward to.'

Toby held my gaze for a moment. 'Are you sure?'

I sighed. 'I honestly don't think that you being a guy, me being a gal, and we having survived a highly pressured end-of-the-world type deal is the basis for a healthy relationship.'

✿ ✿ ✿

JAKE SMITH's writing often focuses on the mundane trivialities and surreal abstractions of human experience through works of poetry, fiction and auto-fiction. He believes that literature works best when its language is playful and malleable; when it is tied to truths yet given the freedom to explore every plane and possibility of that truth.

He is particularly interested in the sounds of language and words, and how musicality is integral to all aspects of our writing. As per Langston Hughes, 'Jazz seeps into words – spelled out words.' This has meant that most of Jake's writing is about jazz and the experience of consuming or creating music whilst he also tries to allude to the processes of music in the textuality of his work; in the sounds and rhythm of his writing and in the appreciation of jazz musicians.

Aside from writing, Jake is a Creative Writing and Education MA student at Goldsmiths University. His primary focuses are in creative forms of education and championing writing that is challenging or experimental. As a poet and short story writer, he believes that creative writing can liberate concepts and narratives which can have innovative and positive effects on society, pushing a new generation of writing. He has an essay and some activities published in Goldsmiths University's "Inspire Anthology" – a collection of writing about creative writing practices of benefit to creative writers and their teaching.

EXPERIENCES DURING LOCKDOWN

During Lockdown, Jake was lucky enough to be able to move in with his family in Shropshire, away from the hustle of London, where he lives, studies and works. He managed to get out regularly in the countryside, went on long walks and bike rides and spent more time focusing on writing poetry, which he had struggled to do in the calamity and constant stir of the capital.

He understands the privilege he had which made this possible and realises that many were not lucky enough to escape first-hand consequences of the pandemic.

Jake has found solace in writing, reading and listening and hopes that others too have had, or can have, similar experiences.

THE KISSA
Jake Smith

Fleeing Tuna Tin City

The snow-capped bumps
on a coffee stained atlas
scuff up my boots
so I swap them for canvas trainers when I arrive
                              back at the hostel
                        in tuna-tin city
                  causing smog dirt in nostrils
                        and mud beneath
                        the white of my nails
                  my lungs tarred and scarred
                        with the smoke I inhaled

            and questions of existence?
            and   belonging?
            and   where to go next?

   sends me to bed early with a tightening chest
      so I listen to jazz – Thelonious Monk
         (Monk's Dream – Take 8)

                  .
            and life

                  .
         slows down

                  .

211

with jazz.

.

Calmer; heart beats slower (81 bpm); closed eyes.

Within this slumber
where my conscious lies broke,
between shrapnels of reality
a solitary sound floats.

A whimper? No. Much louder
yet still gentle upon ear drum stroke.
"A dissonant vibrato";
an instrumentalist would note;
"Through woodwind reeds."
Saxophone? Could be.

As soft as hands and lips
as she felt to me.
Perhaps it's solo for melodic effect
or is it a cry for more harmony?

"Music is the science or
art
of ordering tones or sounds in succession, in combination and
in

temporal relationships
to produce a
composition of unity."

"Psychological effects of
music, sex and drugs
engage the limbic system,
the centre of all emotions."

I flee from the hostel
in wide-eyed hysterics
searching for meaning (and harmony)
in foreign alphanumerics that are
contorting and morphing into lines
that need sorting
or snorting;
          absorbing;
                    deporting;
                              transporting;
so where the fuck is this train that I'm
boarding?

1

'How much of a Jaco fan are you, Habiki?' I asked, tapping my cigarette and swirling my whiskey. I was still unsure on the rules in a Jazz Kissa and started to regret my decision to break the silent trance that the last hour of Santana's "Moonflower" had lured us into.

Habiki took a deep crackling drag, as though he was to embark on a lengthy, liquor-lipped monologue.

'I prefer James Brown,' he croaked in an exhale of smoke, stubbing out his cigarette.

A faded black and white photo of Jaco Pastorius hung above the bar, dangling from a nail and layered with ashen fragments of neglect. Of course, Jaco's relevance had denominated "The Chicken" but from the hand-written door sign and the unkempt memorabilia, he didn't appear to be much cared for.

'James Brown?'

'Yes, boy, James Brown.'

Habiki was rolling a cigarette paper between his thumb and forefinger, manipulating the tobacco into an even spread.

' ... Mister Dynamite; the Godfather of Funk; Soul Brother Number One ... '

'Yeah, man, I know who James Brown is.'

He licked the paper and, with a flick of his right wrist, produced an immaculate roll. He placed it down alongside his lighter and gave me one of his omniscient smirks. Fingering through his James Brown vinyls, he slid the record from the sleeve and placed it upon the turntable. He deftly raised the pin with his pinky and dropped it wonderfully exact into the break between the second and third track. The needle bounced upon the grooves with a whisper.

There it was. That ever so familiar bassline. Saturated by mellowing age yet raw, so raw. It trickled beneath my skin, causing hairs to arise in ovation. The drums pounded at my feet in rhythm, my heel thumped down on the off-beat. And the brass, oh that brass, clung to me, to my ear-drums for as long as the note lasted before it ricocheted away.

'You see?' smirked Habiki, 'James Brown did it first, Pee Wee Ellis composed it for the B side of "The Popcorn".'

'Then why don't you have James Brown above your bar?'

'Daiki. He was much more of a Jaco fan.'

'Daiki?'

He lit his cigarette and nodded, staring through the floorboards, taking long, heavy sucks of smoke. I was confused but decided to stop asking questions.

~

The muffled crackle of the vinyl
warms him.
Like shovelling coal
he fuels the soul,
/the soul train/
with thick white smoke from his nose
and mouth.

Inhaling.
Exhaling.
This magnificent wailing.
The screams of Mr. Dynamite
echo around a flickering lighter,
Shuffling its blue and red flares.

His hairs stand up on their tip-toes.
The funk's in his lymph nodes,
cleaning away
the sadness
of solitude.

~

2

A sprinkling of dust fluttered down from the lampshade and settled in my whiskey glass. Spooning it out with my finger, I watched Mr. Habiki calmly pushing the more expensive liquor to the back of the shelf.

It was simple routine every half an hour or so when trains pulled into platform twelve, causing all four walls of this dim-lit basement to shudder and the whiskey glasses to rattle in tremolo.

Habiki had claimed earlier in the night that this was one of the only authentic Jazz Kissaten left in the city. Many of them had either been bought out by some artisan coffee shop or had been forced to close due to a decline in the popularity of jazz.

Habiki had no doubt been able to stay open due to his location: a tiny basement immediately beneath the city's train station, which undoubtedly cost him a relatively small amount in bills. Customers such as me would stumble upon the place in the fresh hours of the morning, needing a glass of liquor in a panicked hysteria.

We were the only two people remaining in the Kissaten as James Brown provided heartfelt melodies of lost love and black-struggle. "Home Again" was one of my favourites; it was a hiatus from the mainly disco-funk lathered "Get up offa' that thing" LP. James's raspy voice fluttered above the soulful blues ballad.

217

Habiki poured us both another glass full of whiskey and leant back in his armchair. Its leather quilting had stretched and sagged, producing brown wrinkles upon the arms where he balanced a whiskey glass upon one, ashtray upon the other.

I imagined Habiki once smooth-skinned and freshly shaven in his youth. He sat in an identical position, his chair also yet to be wrinkled by age. I could smell the earthy sweetness of the fresh leather. I pictured him smirking ear to ear in exuberance, occasionally tipping his head back in roars of laughter and coughing on his smoke. This was a strange vision to have of a man who I had barely conversed with, but perhaps because I had spent so long solitary in his company and with so little engagement, I was starting to create my own version of him, in a parallel smoother-skinned world.

To me, Habiki seemed as if he were a troubled man; his wrinkles bared signs of pained memories, scars you notice upon an elderly man when reminiscing about his war effort. This Kissaten was Habiki's trench where he lay poised with his turntable and a tin of roll-ups.

'So, how long have you been here?'

Habiki fired smoke from the edge of his pursed lips and ashed.

'Probably around thirty-five years, boy.'

Why did he distance himself from me, intimidating me, reducing me? Because of my youth?

He stood up and searched for another record.

'And had you ... you ... uhhh ... ' I lost my train of thought and started to panic. 'Had you always wanted to open a Kissaten?' I cringed.

'No, I wanted to be a cook, a chef, when I was young.'

'Oh really? How did you end up starting a Jazz Kissa?'

He pulled out a record – Oscar Peterson, "Night Train".

'I didn't open this place.'

I went to fill the gap with a further question – but Habiki beat me to it.

'I would visit here quite often.' His back still turned. 'To avoid the city. It can be a cruel place for some of us. Especially in those days.'

He lifted the pin from the James Brown record, replacing it with the Oscar Peterson. Rumbling piano absorbed the room.

'I was working in a restaurant around the corner.' He was unexpectedly elaborating. 'The ... um ... ah, I forget the name ... quite a fancy place though, Teppanyaki-style.'

'Teppanyaki?'

'Where they cook on a griddle in front of you, on a large round table.'

'Oh, yeah.'

'I would come here after work, usually late, and drink whiskey and smoke. It was the only place I knew that basically stayed open all night.'

My vision of Habiki suddenly altered, shifted direction. He was no longer sitting, laughing in the quilted leather armchair, but on the black sofa, in the far corner of the basement, alone. It disturbed me, as if I had just been told that a memory I had obtained for years wasn't true. I was frustrated with him, as though he had lied to me.

'So, you ended up buying the place out?'

He swerved my query. It seemed that I had provoked him.

'I used to come here, maybe three or four nights a week depending on what shifts I was working. It was an escape for me.'

'An escape from what?'

'The hostel.'

He poured himself extra liquor; he was gradually getting more inebriated.

'I lived with ten other trainee chefs, all boys. We shared a dorm in a hostel but I was never really accepted by them.'

The record slipped onto the third track. A fluid trill upon the high notes wandered up and down the scale before settling into the motif above a brush swept snare. I recognised it. "Georgia on my Mind". I imagined Peterson's large shoulders hunched over the keys, the stage candle-lit in a smoky New York jazz cellar. I wheezed in the smoke.

'They could tell I was different; which they

thought was amusing, I guess. At night I would lie and seal my eyes shut, pretending I was asleep, but I would often hear them talking about me.'

'Why? What would they say about you?' I realised I might have been a bit too personal, so offered to retract. 'Sorry, I don't mind if you don't want to ... '

'No, no, it's fine.' He smiled sympathetically. 'I wasn't quite as ... uhhhh ... ' Habiki searched for his next word in the ember of his cigarette, '... masculine.'

I swallowed my whiskey. 'So you would come here to seek refuge?'

'Yeah, sure, if that's what you want to call it.' He forced a smile then returned his gaze towards the floorboards, hiding his expression behind the mist he let rise from his lips. I watched as he rubbed smoke from his eye with the base of his palm.

I saw a person who had escaped from a world in which he didn't feel welcome. He had sheltered beneath a passing population that had snoozed by on bullet trains or fled from platform twelve, arrived on platform two, commuted daily from five. They had lived beneath the same patch of sky for maybe minutes or generations: drudged in sweat in the rice fields, bumbled on blistered boots from the looming volcanic mass, slumped behind computer screens in asbestos offices, standing solitary in front of desk-filled classrooms.

It was rather significant, at the time, how Habiki and I had both filtered through tuna-tin city, slipped beneath the drains, and concealed ourselves, sinking into the cracked leather of the Kissaten.

We sat bunkered, irrespective of the time or actions of the dayglow streets outside and listened; occupied our brainwaves by following basslines and tempo on course to nothing but the appreciation of the present.

The colours of sound
filled the blank passing of time
where there was nothing.

'What you writing?'

I looked up from my notebook where I had attempted to fill a page with some simple haiku of my travels.

I had always found it hard to describe such moments within syllabic restraints. At university, a tutor had once explained to me the importance of giving yourself a constraint to adhere to; the idea that forcing yourself to keep within the boundaries of a box gave you the freedom and ability to explore every space and corner within those lines, concentrating your creativity. At the time, I had dismissed it as nothing more than the paradoxical rhetoric of an academic who has spent way too long cooped up within a university. However, I was coming round to the idea of exploring this box, probably because I had spent an immeasurable amount of time in this dingy basement and felt as if this restraint had entered physical embodiment. As well as becoming rather drunk. And philosophical.

'Haiku, well ... trying.'

'Read it, loud.' He leant back and tipped his glass up to his lips.

'Umm, I dunno. I'm not too good at writing haiku ... I ... '

'Read!'

I anxiously murmured some of my haiku to him, a little shocked from his sudden enthusiasm. He cupped the lower half of his chin and appeared to become disengaged as he let my words pass through him.

'Good, boy, good.' He was belittling me. 'You complicate things. Haiku is supposed to be ... '

' ... simple, yes, I know but I think ... '

His glare cut through me, piercing my speech.

'You don't need to stick to 5-7-5; it's fucking overcomplicating the simplicity.' He stumbled upon the pronunciation. He was definitely drunk.

Habiki became Gary Snyder to my Kerouac; or perhaps he was Japhy Ryder and I was Ray Smith in some sort of fictional illusion of *The Dharma Bums*.

He stubbed his cigarette and snatched my notebook from me.

'Okay. I mean those are only pretty basic attempts.'

'You see, your version of haiku is based on western syllables, right?'

'Yeah, I guess.'

He scribbled over my writing. 'Traditional haiku is based on Japanese sounds – *on*.'

Habiki explained how such words as Tokyo, which is three syllables to the western ear, actually contains four *on* in Japanese. He broke down the western convention of Haiku in its 5-7-5 form with aggression, stating that it was 'a violation of the haiku form rather than a preservation of it.' He emphasised the importance of the kireji, or cutting word, separating the stanza into its two rhythmical sections.

I sat silent, acting as though I was listening in agreement (in which I mostly was) but my mind wandered past the rhetoric of an intoxicated, agitated man to discover a lonely, fatigued human, rattled in a cage of paranoia by a world that had dismissed him.

' ... and so, it is important to keep true to the simplicity of haiku, through nature and the seasons, as it is the only feature which can truly be translated into western poetry.'

I smiled and tried to move the conversation away from Haiku. 'I'm actually thinking of writing a book which consists of prose and poetry. It would, I guess, explore the lines between poetry and prose, and speech and writing; sound and vision, music and art.'

Habiki nodded. 'Where is the story going to come from?'

'That's it.'

'What is?'

'I mean, nothing happens, really. There will be sections of engaging conversation, and the author will raise thought-provoking topics, but its substance will be found rooted in the narrator's introspective process. It will be like a work of neo-expressionism, or jazz perhaps?'

The Oscar Peterson record hissed as the pin found its way past the final track.

Habiki seemed intrigued by my conversation for the first time as he began to articulate something of a smile. 'Compare this work to say ... ummm ... Peterson. Yes, Peterson. Why not?'

'Nah, not Peterson.' I clicked a lighter to where I balanced a cigarette, pursed between my lips; inhaled deep.

'Do you have that Ellington, Coltrane LP?'

'Their collaborative album?'

'Yeah.'

'I think so.'

3

A quarter of an hour or so had consisted of me trying to justify my comparison through a drunken and impromptu analysis of the LP. I suggested how my piece would also be somewhat of a collaboration between two individuals. I felt as if I had entered a room with Ellington and Coltrane and I was improvising the lead – a tongued jazz of literary comparison with a work yet to be composed. Habiki didn't look like he was following.

It was this acute alcoholism which gave me the courage to politely interrogate Habiki some more, seeing that he was to become a significant character in my writing. I wondered how he had acquired this Kissaten. Why had he chosen to isolate himself here?

'Who managed this Kissa before you?'

'Daiki.'

He had mentioned Daiki previously.

'Ah. So, how did you inherit it from him?'

'It's complicated.'

He began to roll up another cigarette. What must have been around his twentieth. I was obliged to follow suit, although it disturbed me to think how many carcinogens must have passed through his respiratory system. As if he had no care for his health. Was it merely his addiction to nicotine or possibly his only perceived escape from the Kissa?

A simplistic but protracted suicide. He would watch the smoke rise up and disperse, its once dense, gaseous molecules separating from their thick, white embodiment to the point where they were no longer visible to the human eye. The particles integrated into the atmosphere around us in an invisible and tranquil grace.

'I didn't smoke before I met him.' Possibly he noticed my concerned expression as he inhaled. 'Daiki was an enthusiastic smoker. He talked of the mindfulness benefits. He thought he would go insane if he stopped – a kind of zen.'

'As if smoking is a form of meditation?'

'Yes. He would say that he would be able to enter a zen state of mind in the five or so minutes of his smoke. It's the act of breathing, and the ability to slow life down for a short period of time and contemplate.'

'I suppose I see where he was coming from.' I lit my cigarette and savoured the first drag, trying to picture Daiki.

'If it wasn't for smoking, he would have succumbed to some other disease or disorder.'

I exhaled. 'Did he die from it?'

'From what?'

'A smoking habit?'

'He was sick. Sick in the lungs. We weren't quite sure what it was.'

'He wasn't diagnosed?'

'No, he refused to go see a doctor. He didn't want

to know.' He squinted in thought. 'He would say "Waiting for luck or waiting for death? What's the difference?" or something near to that when translated into your strange language. So, we spent our last few weeks in here, playing records.'

'I'm sorry.'

'Don't be sorry, it's not as hard as you think.' He hid behind his smoke again.

'What isn't?'

'Saying a final goodbye to someone you love. You know, if you're prepared for it, it's kind of relieving.'

I imagined Daiki's particles dispersing into the air of the Kissa, integrating into the atmosphere. As if he were still here, but just a part of something much greater than the lung-tarred human he once embodied.

'Yeah, I can imagine. I've never really had to.'

I didn't know what else to say, so I filled the awkward silence with puffs on my cigarette.

I recalled life at home. Fresh from university, I was desperately searching for some sort of stability to grasp onto; but I had denied this and instead exported myself far across the world, hoping to avoid any responsibility.

I felt intimidated and oppressed by my parents' expectations (they wanted me to fall into some safe journalism job) but, also, largely by a global agenda that forced roles upon humankind; expecting us to find 'the perfect job' to serve each other's materialistic needs.

Humanity was collectively impoverishing those without a voice; whether it be plants and animals, or other homo-sapiens alike, disadvantaged and disenfranchised in undermined countries and even neighbourhoods. Still, the clouds above this calamity are contaminated with acid.

I longed for life to be simpler again – to be unaware or distracted. I longed for companionship.

'Are you in love?'

Startled by the plain simplicity of his interrogation, I coughed on my smoke.

'Umm, I have been, I guess, yeah.' Deflecting a yes or no response.

I had never been comfortable talking to people about love. I would squirm at the possibility of having to address clichés or confess a deep emotion, conditioned to believe that I must hide behind masculinity; 'man up!' But perhaps I didn't want to be so vulnerable. I was obliged, however, to open myself up to Habiki.

The Dance Floor

Squeaky soles of sticky trainers.
Soul trainers.
Lamers, onlookers
alone by the side,
no brainers.
'Cus my trainers are twisting, turning, gyrating.

'I
   Need
       A
          Piss'

The front. The ear popping
speaker.
My trembling beer beaker.
Her blonde hair is swooshing,
star-sequined dress grooving.
Sets her free, does not contain her.
Her trainers
black with dance dirt
in all the right places.
Spaces.

'I
   Need
       A
          Cig'

Chuckles between puffs,
some discreet snuffs and huffs.
Deep deep drags.

Offbeat acquaintances
will nod out their hi-ya's,
as no talk will transpire.
Hoisting their brows
with inelegant strings.

'I
 Need
   To
     Dance'

Back on the floor my trainers
come loose at the bases.
No space in this place
to bend down and tie laces.
'Cus upon this dance-floor,
it's so easy to ignore
the disparities between us.

Our soles squeak one sound,
upon sticky dance ground.
Emancipating trainers of all types,
your Adidas; his Nikes.
Accumulating floor filth
inside my head.

'Let's
    Go
       To
          Mine'

I scratch the inky freckles of dance dirt,
from the softness of her skirt,
yet still find more
speckled upon pale sheets.
She locks the door.
The tinnitus pierces like razors.

I slip off my trainers.

Habiki filled up our glasses. He instructed me to have a look through his records and select one of my choice. I took my time, as if this were to be the final record we would hear together, in our collaboration. By the time I found it, Habiki had fallen into a deep liquor-infused coma. I slipped the record out of the sleeve and placed it on the turntable, turning down the volume so as not to wake him.

I picked out "Bitches Brew": the pioneering Miles Davis album that re-liquefied the formerly congealed jazz era into a psychedelic soup of cross-genre procreation. By throwing any preconception of rhythm and harmony out of a Midtown Manhattan top floor window, Miles leapt between two Astral planes of jazz and rock; single-handedly soldering jazz-fusion into the mainstream, whilst employing his other hand to pinch ear-drum-skin with the valves of his horn.

I knew a great amount about this album, my fascination with Davis peaking in my late teens, during the early years of my jazz awakening. I had spent many evenings getting high in dim-lit attic rooms, drinking cans of Holsten and inhaling cheap, nasty incense – before settling on Nag Champa for a more consistent choke – listening to Davis and his innovative affiliates: Bill Evans, Coltrane, Wayne Shorter, Herbie Hancock. Often sharing this appreciation through hazy discourse about the beauty of jazz improvisation and masterfulness and later discussing how time is merely a concept, or how likely it is that we unconsciously exist in a simulation and whether we actually have free will or if our actions are simply the unfolding effect of our genetics.

This was the first time I had seen "Bitches Brew" in its full LP glory. It was weighty in my hands and brought my appreciation for the album into the physical.

The cover art was expressionistic, depicting a couple embracing and looking out upon the tranquillity of the sea, despite the tempestuous clouds and lightning above. The calm being the comfort of Sixties jazz, the peace of accepted jazz forms and structures; and the storm being the fearless electricity of Miles and his astral journey into jazz fusion, a ferocious revolution in music production – the use of the new technique of looping.

I noticed the female's hair becoming distressed and smudged into the clouds by the psychedelia of flower power that folded out onto the reverse. The two sides were juxtaposed by inverting the day blue sky on the front with the cosmic darkness of space; foregrounded by an anguished Zulu goddess. A rather busy portrayal of Miles Davis's transition into the seventies.

I began to wonder about the title "Bitches Brew";

slightly derogatory? Yet common terminology in the African-American dialect of the era; so, did this make it okay?

Probably not? I wasn't sure. The absence of the apostrophe in "Bitches" confirmed that "Brew" was not a noun but a verb; suggesting that the "Bitches", whoever they were, were cultivating some sort of substance? Or co-ordinating a movement? Perhaps an uprising from being degraded under the said term? Although it was possibly a cultural play on the words "witches' brew" where, within such a cauldron, Miles would stir his psychedelic soup.

Inside the fold of the LP was a short essay worth of liner notes, written by the philosophical music critic, Ralph J. Gleason. It was beautifully under-punctuated which gave the writing a sort of improvised flow, replicating Davis's lawless style.

A particular section provoked me: *They make this music like they make those poems and those pictures and the rest because if they do not they cannot sleep nor rest nor, really, live at all. This is how they live, the true ones, by making art which is creation.*

I began concluding: where morphemes meet rhythm that meets lips to speak poetry, it relies on you, the listener, and your sonic engagement and subsequent emotion to measure its success as a poem. You must embark on a vivid journey of similes and metaphors, following the poet's often subliminal prompts which decide where you place your feelings throughout. Lips move faster, louder, an intense passion is pursued through rapid rhythms of rhyme and syllabic suspense.

This is a similar experience with jazz. Once the needle is placed upon the grooves and a comfortable position is occupied – pillows propped up against the back of the bed, the attic-window slightly ajar, the click of a lighter and ensuing emanation of the incense stick – you, the listener, also begin a similar subliminal journey.

Waves of intensity: from double bass to shrill screaming trumpet and loose hi-hat hiss gives you sweaty hands and an increased heart rate; glimmers of harmonic hopes that the first theme might return are shattered with a modal guitar solo which ships you to a completely different emotional environment than you expected – the lighting in the room looks different. The texture thins out; rolled out flat with a looped bassline and elongated horn; *calmer; heart beats slower (81bpm).* Soft bongo beats, a spoonful of zen serenity. A spiritual journey concludes in a convulsive crescendo of crashed cymbals, leaving you temporarily disengaged with reality, lingering on the final stanza or note.

In a brushstroke, the art of poetry is much the same as the art of jazz. It relies on the listener's response and interpretation. I took a long retrospective sip. Habiki was still asleep. I'd probably had enough whiskey, I thought.

5

It takes some simple social skills to know when to part from someone's company. Nevertheless, during my time with Habiki, which had lasted till the break of morning light, I did not feel inclined to leave. In fact, I could not imagine how I would say my goodbyes to him – shake his hand? Would I embrace him with a hug? – because the future that was ahead of us (specifically *this* future), where I would eventually take my leave, seemed to have lost any significance inside the Kissa.

The appreciation of the present was more justifiable. I had discovered how my mind was plagued with plans and compulsions to fill future timelines. In a world where we are fed hundreds of narratives a day through LCD projections, it had been easy for me to get lost in a mist of half-read articles and status updates. I planned to focus on the narrative immediately in front of me, with the Kissa being the juncture, the critical moment of the narrative, where everything changed.

It was rude to walk out into the morning sun and abandon Habiki without some sort of goodbye. So, I rolled up a cigarette; took my time smoothing the tobacco into an even spread. I watched the paper ignite; expanded out to my fingertips, cupping the red lighter. Further up my arm, I expanded, noticing the glimmering glow of my skin beneath the amber burn of the cigarette. Expanded further, to my head and chest, then down to my legs; felt autonomy from the chains of my anxieties. I expanded outwards further, saw the Kissa beneath me, where I sat, inhaling deep into thoughts and visions. Habiki sat slouched and slumbered in his cracked leather, fingers twitching. Further, further.

Now I saw the city in a diorama; trains meandered beneath the salmon pink of morning sky, slinking through platform twelve. I had perspective. Mortal specks of flesh and fabric descended the volcano, swapping scuffed up boots for canvas trainers, euphoric from the vantage upon which they perceived their perfect view of the city. Little did they know of the outlook from the Kissa. They had all been so close: arriving in the station and fleeing towards the city, towards the hostels and restaurants and bars and hiking trails. Ha! If only they'd known what they could have seen, had they dug a little deeper, beneath their obsession with the future.

I expanded further, advancing past the ozone layer; deeper, deeper, darker, darker, into the atmosphere, when I perceived a familiar noise. *A whimper? No, much louder yet still gentle upon ear drum stroke.* The earth rotated slowly. The further I expanded, the louder it became, almost deafening. The music of nothingness, emptiness, poured into ears of acceptance.

❋ ❋ ❋

CLAIRE WILSON is an aspiring crime writer from Falkirk, Scotland. She is currently seeking representation for her seven-book crime series which she has spent the last ten years writing.

EXPERIENCES DURING LOCKDOWN

Lockdown has made Claire confront her feelings of loneliness and other things she is unhappy about within her life. She has made a list of the realistic things she can change to combat this.

Claire has been employed by the Scottish Prison Service for almost twenty years and has been required at work during the Lockdown period. Not being able to see family members was tough but being at work gave her a sense of normalcy which made Lockdown more bearable.

Claire's work within the Prison Service is why she is drawn to writing about crime.

BRAINS
Claire Wilson

'I love her big tits,' joked Krissy.

I tried not to take offence. If Chloe, my girlfriend, had picked him instead of me, I would've been jealous too. It would be better if my mates didn't speak about her at all. It only got us in trouble. But Krissy didn't possess a social filter.

Mum was convinced Chloe was too young for me, as if that mattered. It was only a year, not three as there was between her and dad. She had a cheek to voice her opinion. It was nothing to do with her. With anyone.

Apparently, I'd changed since I started seeing Chloe. Mum didn't understand that I was growing up. She couldn't control me anymore and hated it. I'd missed some school? So what? I couldn't learn anything new now. If I decided to sit my exams, I'd pass them.

I wanted Chloe and me to move into our own place where we could be alone, with no interference from anybody. But to do that, I needed money. A proper job didn't appeal to me.

Krissy got another round in, ignoring that I'd said I didn't want any more shots. It was his way of getting to me without it being obvious. Ronnie would hit him if he noticed it. Krissy at his worst when he was drinking. The best time to talk to him was when he was hungover. He didn't answer back then.

I sent a text to mum to prevent her from pestering me when it was past ten o'clock. At seventeen, she thought ten p.m. was still an acceptable curfew.

Staying at Ronnie's – see you tomorrow! I didn't add any kisses nor wait for a response.

Life was too short to be moaned at. With that in mind, I picked up the shot glass and downed it.

'Calm doon, Brains,' said Ronnie. 'I'm no carryin' yie hame and you better no spew in ma flat again.'

My cheeks blazed at the memory.

'Aye, Brains,' mimicked Krissy.

Ronnie silenced him with a withering look. A small victory for me.

They called me Brains because I was supposed to be intelligent. But I hated school, I hated learning, I hated exams.

Life was for having fun with friends and spending time with my girlfriend. Ronnie had put me in touch with some of his contacts. I dropped off packages in exchange for cash. I wasn't stupid. I knew what the packages contained. But it was easy money, especially with my pushbike.

We played a few games of pool until it was time to go to the club. I hoped Chloe was there, that she was dressed appropriately. I didn't want guys drooling over her. The thought made me clench my jaw until my temple ached. Anger surged up inside me, leaving me breathless.

'Is everything okay, fella?' asked Ronnie as he potted the black.

'Aye.'

'Yie want a line?'

I nodded and the three of us drained our drinks and headed to the Gents. With damp palms, I rubbed my nose in anticipation.

Ronnie produced his stash, pouring enough for three fat lines on the cistern. Krissy provided a banknote and rolled it up like a straw. He stepped forward, but Ronnie put a hand on his chest.

'Brains is first.'

A flash of anger passed though Krissy's eyes, disappearing before it fully registered.

I plucked the note and soaked up the nearest line. My nostril temporarily stung as the powder shot up into me. I rolled my head back and gasped.

'Here we fuckin' go,' I roared.

Ronnie laughed but Krissy looked disgusted. I passed the note to Ronnie.

'Yer acting as if you've never had a bit of Charlie afore,' muttered Krissy under his breath as he waited his turn.

I ignored him. My confidence, my mood, my excitement, everything was rising.

While Krissy was taking his line, I grabbed my mobile and dialled Chloe's number. It rang. And rang. Voicemail.

'Chloe, it's Brains. Where the fuck are yie? Who're yie wi? Why aren't yie answering the phone?' I paused until I had caught my breath. 'Love yie, right?'

'Woman trouble?' asked Krissy, as he wiped his nose. 'Don't cry, Brains. Maybe she's found herself a real man.'

I pushed him into the urinal.

'What the fuck are yie playing at?' he shouted.

Ronnie intervened before Krissy could land any punches.

'Calm doon, the pair of yie. Fucking kids. Now,' sniffed Ronnie, 'come on, ladies. Kiss and make up.'

It was full dark and the rain had started. We pulled our jackets a little tighter and kept our heads down.

The queue to get in the club went round the building and down the next street. The queue didn't bother Ronnie though; he walked right up to the Bouncers and they let us in. Some were the biggest drug dealers in town. Most worked for Ronnie.

We went straight to the cloakroom and handed in our Stone Island and North Face jackets to the clerk.

Once our jackets were stored, we took the stairs to enter the main club. The stench of stale urine and beer mingled together. The throbbing beat bounced against my body and the thrill of excitement overwhelmed me.

'Yie dancin', Brains?' asked Ronnie as he nudged

my arm. 'Krissy away and get the drinks in, we're going fanny huntin' in the club.'

We walked out onto the dance floor to teach these women how to dance. One of them tried to kiss me but I gently pushed her away.

'I'm a one-woman man,' I crooned in her ear.

She quickly moved onto Ronnie when she realised I wasn't interested. Ronnie wasn't a good-looking lad. The knife marks on his cheek and forehead didn't help, which pulled his lips into a permanent scowl.

'I deserve them, Brains,' he explained to me one day. 'I deserve every scar I've got.' He'd done more damage than had ever been inflicted on him.

I saw Chloe before she saw me. She was wearing a slinky green dress that hung over her right shoulder. Her long brown hair was curled the way I liked. She looked stunning and ten years older than she was, helped by the Jimmy Choos I got her for Christmas. They were real ones too – nothing cheap for my girl!

I watched her for several seconds, talking to her friends and gesticulating whilst holding a tumbler that I knew would contain vodka and cola, her favourite drink.

'There's ma girl,' I shouted over to Ronnie.

He nodded his head in acknowledgement but made no move to follow me, too busy with the one who was giving him attention.

I walked over to Chloe and put my arm around

her shoulders. My chest heaved with pride when she reached up and gave me a deep kiss. I hoped Krissy was watching.

'Hi, Brains,' said Nicole.

I didn't have any time for her. She led Chloe astray. I wished she'd stop hanging around with her.

'How's yer night been?' interjected Chloe, trying to stem the tension. She knew I'd be annoyed.

'Aye, good. Better noo you're here. Yie been in long?'

'Aboot half an hour or so.'

'Anybody been giving yie any hassle?' She rolled her eyes at me.

'No, Billy.'

I must have annoyed her. She only used my real name when she was annoyed with me. She knew I hated it, but I was in too good a mood to let it bother me.

I badly wanted another line of coke. I tried to get Ronnie's attention, but his tongue was down the other girl's throat.

He kept his stash in a vial in his wallet. I could help myself. He wouldn't mind if I slipped my fingers in-between the black leather wallet and the fabric of his denim jeans. Before I had the chance to grasp the wallet, he spun around, seconds away from punching me.

'Brains, man – whit the fuck?'

'Sorry, mate. I wanted a wee bit of powder.'

'Then ask, ya mad man.'

We left Krissy with the girls, holding the drinks. The idiot.

'You're a greedy bastard.'

Tears were streaming down my face – a combination of laughing and the sting of the cocaine against my nostril.

'I hope that wee bird's still waiting for yie,' I said as we inspected our nostrils for any stray powder.

'She's a wee dirty. I'm sure Krissy's already hud her. She's probably cracking onto someone else.'

'Is it okay if Chloe comes back with me to yours? She'll behave.'

He watched me, stared at me, as if I was a puzzle he was trying to figure out.

'Answer me, then.'

'Do you trust her?'

'Aye,' I replied with zero hesitation. 'Why yie askin'?'

'Di yie really wanty ken?'

'Aye, obviously.'

'I've heard a few whispers.'

'Whispers aboot whit?' I interrupted.

'Aboot Chloe.'

'Whit?'

My heart seized, as it did the first time I took cocaine. Almost as if my heart had stopped and had been restarted by those electric things they put on your chest in hospital. "Clear", my mind shouted, "Clear".

I didn't want to hear the words that were about to leave his lips but, at the same time, I couldn't hear them fast enough.

'See that day we went fishin' and we ended up stayin' ernight?' I nodded. 'Well, I heard fae a few reliable people she shagged Lawrence at a pairty.'

'What? Lawrence Daniels?'

'Aye.'

'Why are yie tellin' me this noo? How long've ye kent about this? Yer supposed to be ma best pal.'

'I swear down I only heard yesterday.'

I didn't want to cry in front of Ronnie, but the tears were there.

'That'll be right fae her.'

'Don't git upset er her. She's no worth it.'

She was though. She was my girl.

'All birds are hoors. The earlier yie find that oot, the better.'

I wanted to lie down on the dirty, sticky toilet floor and weep.

I stormed out of the toilets and marched over to the dance floor. She had this stupid drunken grin on her face which said she was pleased to see me. I wanted to knock the smile off her face. How dare she embarrass me. And with one of my enemies too. Bitch.

'Oi ya wee cow. Is it true?'

'Whit are ye talkin' aboot?'

'You and Lawrence. Don't even try and deny it, ya slag. Do yie hink ahm fuckin' stupid? Yie shagged

247

him.'

'I never did.'

'LIAR,' I screamed.

'Calm doon,' said Krissy. 'You'll get us kicked oot.'

'I don't give a fuck,' I answered.

'Hae a drink,' suggested Ronnie. 'Mebbe yie should go hame, hen. Until he calms doon.'

'No. Ahv no done anything. Mebbe Billy should go hame.'

I knocked the drink out of her hand.

'Hink yer a big girl 'cos yer drinkin' in a club?'

She stared at me, her mouth open.

'Is it true?' I begged. 'Tell me.'

'I'm no even answerin' that. Yie clearly wanty believe it. Grow up, Brains.'

'Answer me,' I screamed.

People around us stopped. Ronnie gave them his trademark growl and they hastily turned back to their own business. My fingers itched to grab her by the throat and give her a shake. Shake that disgusted expression off her face.

'Ahm no scared of you like everyone else is. Noo fuck off. Yer ruining ma night oot.'

I glanced at Ronnie to gauge his reaction. I watched, hypnotised, as his jaw clenched several times. I knew from experience he'd be trying hard to compose himself.

'Let's go, wee man, afore ah do somehing I'll regret.'

'Aye, fuck off,' shouted Chloe.

We grabbed our jackets and exited the club. I shoved my cold hands in my pockets to keep them warm.

'She's a tart. A wrong yin. I ken it hurts but yer better off awa fae her. Trust me.'

We stopped so that Ronnie could spark up a cigarette.

'She dun it,' he added as he exhaled blue smoke.

'Shut up. SHUT UP.'

His words assaulted me worse than any blade could.

'Yie need to hear it. I bet yie any money she'll leave that club wi a guy the night. Any money.'

'Aye. We left her wi Krissy. He'll try and fire into her. I'll kill him if he does,' I muttered.

Without saying another word, Ronnie pulled his mobile out of his back pocket and dialled a number as we continued to walk up the main road.

'Where are yie?' he said into the phone. Brutal.

Without waiting for any explanation, he ended the call and slipped the phone back into his pocket. If the cold was affecting him, he didn't show it. We walked on for a few more minutes before Krissy caught up, panting from his run.

'I didny ken where yie went,' he explained when his breath returned.

'Whit was she saying when we left?' I asked.

'She said if yie didny trust her, it was over, and yie were a ugly wee poof.'

Now it was my turn to clench my jaw. Ronnie threw him a dirty look, as if he was disgusted that Krissy hadn't lied and had kept quiet instead of infuriating me further.

'Don't worry,' soothed Ronnie. 'We'll dust that Lawrence on sight.'

I nodded. No matter what, he had my back.

'Come oan,' he added, 'we'll go ti the shop and get some drink to take back to mine.'

That meant he wanted to stay up all night, drinking and taking Charlie. I hoped he had more in his house. I wanted to feel numb. To feel nothing. We would have a party ourselves. Who needed a nightclub with their overpriced drinks? Fuck that. At least this way I'd save money.

We walked along the street in silence. I was too angry to talk, and Krissy was too scared to annoy Ronnie any further.

I concentrated on my trainers, on putting one foot in front of the other as we made our way to the off-licence.

'Oi, ya c...,' cried Ronnie.

I looked up and couldn't believe what I was seeing. It was as if by thinking about him had made him appear in front of me.

Lawrence Daniels.

He had the audacity to stare at us. Even though we were far away, we could see the colour in his face change. He started to run and the three of us gave chase. I heard the metallic click of Ronnie's lock-back knife and was pleased.

Protected.

In the end, it was Krissy who caught up with him first. Krissy had always been the fastest runner, regardless how much drink or drugs he'd had. By the time me and Ronnie reached him, we were both panting loudly and, for a scary second, I thought I was going to be sick. The alcohol was churning around in my stomach, like clothes in a washing machine.

I watched on as Krissy punched Lawrence a few times in the ribs. The force of the violence caused him to fall to his knees. Krissy kept a good hold of him in case he slipped out of his grasp and managed to get away.

'Do him,' screamed Ronnie beside me.

His anger spurned me on.

I needed a fag, but now wasn't the right time. My reputation was at stake. If people knew I'd got Ronnie and Krissy to fight my battles for me, I was done. If I didn't punish him, I was done. All the respect I'd carefully crafted for myself would disappear in seconds. I didn't think that this was somebody's son, brother, uncle, dad. I saw red and had to act.

'Ya bastard,' I shouted. I ran towards him and kicked him as hard as I could in the stomach.

'Get him,' shouted Ronnie.

His words spurred me on. I wanted to make him bleed, I wanted to watch as red liquid seeped from his broken body. Lifting my foot, I kicked him again. Harder. Something cracked under my foot, mirroring the sound of squishing a cockroach on holiday. I was standing on a beast. An insect.

Krissy let go as I kicked Lawrence to the ground. I wanted him to feel what I'd felt in a club toilet that stank of pee, being told my world had collapsed. I wanted his lung to collapse. Tiring, I stopped to catch my breath as Krissy jumped on top of Lawrence's head.

You don't take a guy's girlfriend. It was a code you didn't breach. Lawrence had to be taught a lesson, and it was our duty to pass the message along. In that moment, me, Krissy and Ronnie were united.

I wanted Lawrence to have to piss out of a tube. Every time he wanted to shag a girl, I wanted him to think of me. I wanted to make sure he would never father another child. I concentrated the aim of my kicks between his legs. One kick. Two.

'He's unconscious.' Krissy stopped to catch a breath.

Beside us, Ronnie was quiet; the only sound of his existence was his heavy breathing.

Krissy stopped to light a fag.

'Give us a draw,' I ordered.

Surprised. He handed it over. I took a few puffs before I handed it back to him.

'Ha,' I laughed. 'He's pissed himself.' Then I noticed he had urinated over my shoe.

'Dirty bastard,' I screamed again as I booted him.

He was bleeding, but only in small cuts and bruises. The blood wasn't leaking out of him as I wanted it to.

'Cut him,' I instructed Ronnie.

He didn't reply or even nod his head. He walked towards the body lying broken on the floor. The violence excited him. It didn't matter that he hadn't inflicted any of the blows. Merely watching was sufficient to satisfy his dark fantasies.

'Hold him up,' instructed Ronnie. He was looking at Krissy, so I didn't move.

Without saying a word, Krissy grabbed him beneath his armpits and pulled him up, as if he was sitting on the floor. A puppet. Only thing missing was his strings.

'A little higher,' ordered Ronnie.

Krissy heaved him up. His time spent at the gym had paid off.

Ronnie stood in front of Lawrence, savouring the moment. The knife glinted in his hand against the moonlight. I watched him as he passed it between each of his hands, deep in thought.

My eyes widened in surprise at how easily the knife had slipped into Lawrence's white T-shirt. The red material spooled around the knife and spread as the fabric drank in the red, thick liquid. It was mesmerising to watch the red circle spread over the top. Ronnie had left the knife in, just where he had inserted it. Almost as if he wanted to take a picture. The knife squelched as he slowly pulled it out. It made the blood flow quicker and it began to surround our feet.

Lawrence was frozen. Unmoving. Eyes staring at nothing.

It wasn't until we moved away that I noticed the soles of my trainers were pooled in Lawrence's blood. My nerves caused me to laugh out loud, an enraged hyena.

'Let's go,' suggested Krissy.

Ronnie never moved. He was taking a photograph with his eyes, his mind. Krissy pulled at his arm.

'Let's GO, Ronnie.'

He was in a trance. Wiping the blade of his knife against the tiny part of Lawrence's top that was white, we made our move to get away from the body.

That would teach him. He wouldn't want to shag any guy's girlfriend now. The knife went that deep he would probably be left with a scar. He wouldn't show his face in this part of Glasgow again, I thought, as we continued towards Ronnie's flat.

'We need to get our stories straight,' muttered Krissy.

I wanted to sleep, but Krissy wouldn't let us until he was convinced we were all saying the same thing. We'd left the club and went straight to Ronnie's. Krissy offered to get his friend to confirm he'd given us a lift, but Ronnie said no, finally talking. He didn't want anyone else involved.

I was confused. I wanted everyone to know that we'd been the ones to teach Lawrence a lesson. But they were saying I couldn't tell.

I didn't mention my bloody footprints, fearing Ronnie would be annoyed with me. Krissy took the knife off him, promising to chuck it into the canal behind the flats.

The three of us were connected.

Forever.

ADDITIONAL STORIES EMBRACING
"LOCKDOWN # 1" AND "GENERAL"
THEMES

DETAILS OF BRIAN JOHN FEEHAN
CAN BE FOUND ON PAGE 38

THE NEGATION OF DELUSION
Brian John Feehan

He combed through her deceptions like the tangles in her hair, pausing to tease past each before catching on another.

She had never been a gentle liar, preferring the cataclysmic to the mundane. She hadn't come in past curfew because she had lost track of time, or a friend needed a shoulder on which to cry. No.

She had been stopped on a deserted road by an undercover agent with the FBI, who commandeered her vehicle for a sting operation that was underway though gone awry. But, not to worry, because they had apprehended the kingpin/terrorist/serial killer. As a result, everything was right with the world. Again. And she was home.

And she was home. Safe and sound and at home. So, why the fuss? Why did he have to create so much drama (as if he were the only thespian in the room). And she was always correct, was she not? She stood fine and dandy. The world much better/safer/saner now that the government men had caught their menace. The car was intact. The dog alive. The merchandise returned, and charges dropped.

If these were isolated occurrences, he might have agreed. Sighed the relief of the angels upon her safe return.

But they weren't. Hadn't been since she was a

child. It was almost as if the lies had been born first, and her body formed around them, a chrysalis protecting its precious cargo inside.

The girl's mother was the antithesis of the child that she sired. Each gesture was a whisper, every footfall an apology. Where she was demure, her daughter demurred, spouting her bare and boldfaced tales, the cloth with which she wove her fabrications was whole and absolute.

The vase hadn't broken because of a bump or jostle – something accidental and easily assuaged. A tremor occurred, (somehow only affecting their home), dropping her to the ground, ('it was a wonder I hadn't been crushed'), the vase a mere trifle in what was an otherwise traumatic event. She was only four at the time. A blonde-headed wisp, a demon with dimples, large blue eyes recalling a summer sky after a storm, revealing a day potent with promise.

But the man's wife did not have the resilience to tolerate such onslaughts; her camel's back endured its final straw, and she was gone. In the end, it was, in truth, the lies that set her free. He did not upbraid the woman. He could not blame or fault her. Living with the girl was a test few, if any, could bear. And, as the child grew, so did the falsehoods.

At seven, she claimed to have found dinosaur bones in their yard, breathlessly bragging to her schoolmates that a museum was to be built around their home. She collected entrance fees which she never returned. At twelve, the tales escalated when she devised another fiction: her uncle, (which she did not have), was confined to prison for murder. But he had escaped and was living in her parents' attic, resulting in a visit from the authorities with warrants, as her fabrication, so replete with detail, had made its way to a policeman parent.

Sweet Sixteen found her anything but, creating a Ponzi scheme of sorts at a Senior Center at which she had volunteered. But her ability to spin her subterfuge allowed her to circumvent any recompense.

As an adult, the truth had receded as far from her as a zealot from a zygote. Her deceits were pathological; her frequency, habitual. And now this.

And now this. This was exceptional, even for the girl.

She had been dating the boy for several months. He was sweet, but simple-minded, or, at least, so besotted with her charms as to yet notice how much of what she declared dissembled from reality. Whatever she offered him, he took as gospel, when a shaker of salt would have been preferred. So twisted was he around and about her fingers, he acquiesced to any whim, succumbed to every ask.

Her father was well aware of her endeavors; he had been the recipient of multiple manipulations. Not the boy. If she insisted she could fly, he would spend his day considering the heavens anticipating her approach. If she asserted she could walk on water, he'd be there, patiently waiting upon the shore.

But he believed her once too often, and now she needed daddy to help ameliorate her deceits. Which he had done before, without question or fail. But not this.

But not this. He listened to her mold the myth, unfolding this new fallacy, of how and who and what had befallen. In another time and place, it might have been turned into an epic poem. But this was not another time or place, and what had transpired could not be spun into an alternative type of fiction. He realized this as he contemplated the chaos of crimson in her trunk, the remains and regret of a boy much too trusting.

Grabbing shovel and pick, he tossed them in and drove with her to a spot he knew. A place that until then had occupied memories of August nights and clandestine kisses. All of those would be replaced by this. Not content with the present, her deceits were destroying his remembrances of the past. And still, he dug.

And still, he dug. With her by his side. It was a sizable hole.

For the man had begun to devise some lies of his own.

THE PROTÉGÉ
Brian John Feehan

'Again,' the Maestro commanded. The Pupil responded, repeating the passage for the umpteenth time.

The Pupil was dedicated, deliberate, didactically determined, desperate to please the man who had become his Mentor. When he had repeated the exercise, the Pupil turned to the Maestro and queried, 'Better?' To which the Maestro responded, 'Some ways to go, still. But a definite improvement.'

The Pupil bared his teeth in a simile of a smile, so pleased at the mere mention of merit from the man. The orchestrated arrangement bonding man to boy had been ongoing for several years, with the Maestro serving as both Mentor and Master. All of their time was consumed with the Protégé immersed in learning the Maestro's magnum opus: a thirty-six hour, twelve-minute, and forty-two-second representation of the Maestro's unparalleled genius (at least in his own estimation). It was the longest, non-repetitive piece of music ever written for the solo piano.

Erik Satie created *Vexations*, but this was only one page of music repeated in perpetuity for eighteen hours. Rzewski's *The Road* was ten hours of non-repetition. But the Master had outdone them all. His new composition was based on an epic poem which, by comparison, would make the Mahabharata, the longest prose poem ever written, read like a haiku.

In addition to its length, the work was enormously challenging. In perspective, performing some of the most difficult piano pieces in history such as Scriabin's *Sonata No. 5* or Sorabji's *Opus Clavicembalisticum* was analogous to a toddler playing chopsticks; the Maestro's composition was as chaotic as a torrent on a tin roof or a colloquium of quadratic equations in the key of E. In point of fact, the piece was so complicated and catastrophic that the only other player to attempt it was finally sequestered to a state-run sanitarium.

This was why the Master required the Pupil. Though not yet elderly, as far as the banquet of life was concerned, he was closer to a digestive than an aperitif. He had searched for almost a year, in and out of endless recitals and concert halls, desperate to find the student who could possess the skill, stamina, and soul to transform his creation from simply notes on a page, (hundreds upon hundreds of them), into a thing of epic transcendence.

And then he discovered the boy. A prodigy since birth, the child was giving a concert which the Maestro attended. This seven-year-old lad strode onto the stage clad in shorts and knee socks, a cowlick the only portion of him extending above the keyboard. But when he began to play, the Maestro was transfixed by the boy's ability and passion, and he recognized the immutable truth that he needed to search no further. He had found his Protégé.

The Maestro immediately presented his proposal: the boy would come and live with the man for as long as was necessary to accomplish the task. The Pupil's parents were gratified that someone as eminent as the Maestro would lavish such attention on their son, and willingly accepted the composer's arrangement.

Truth be told, those were trying times. The boy's father had been a weaver, but somehow lost the thread of his life, now spending his days bereft of the weft.

Having one less mouth to feed offered some respite for their little family, as did the trifling stipend the Master offered as recompense for allowing him to take and tutor their boy.

To begin, their partnership was a panto in contrapunto, this aging Major composer with his diminutive Minor charge – not dissonant though distant. But over time, they became a tune in unison, both melodies in harmonic agreement with the other.

The Protégé's parents attempted to visit the lad with regularity – that is, when time permitted. But the boy did not seem to mind that he was an intermittent offspring, as his devotion to the Master was absolute; time spent with the man or his Work was infinitely more rewarding than those spent without. Nothing else was of consequence, not his mother or father or sister; not kisses goodnight or cookies on a tray or a Sunday catch with a baseball and glove.

They took their meals together, the boy and the man. They rehearsed for several arduous hours every morning and, likewise, in the afternoon.

One day per week, the Maestro would take the boy on an educational trip – to magnificent museums or rococo concert halls. Alternately, the Maestro might read aloud from the greatest works of literature. He believed that every form of art nourished the others, and exposure to this excellence would, over time, percolate into the Pupil's own playing. Each night the Maestro would stand as the boy kneeled, reciting his prayers, then tuck him in for his long night's rest – the Maestro watching o'er, as his own Mentor had done before.

The Master's previous attempt at an epic opus, a still-lengthy but nowhere near as robust a composition as his current one, received the most tepid reviews in its debut. *The latest offering reveals flashes of brilliance followed by eternities of banality.*

In an effort to turn lemons into an acceptable drink, *Eternities of Banality* was what the Master had originally entitled both the poem and the new work that the boy was so diligently deciphering. But fearing he might be tempting the fates, he amended the title to *Vesuviana*.

The Pupil had yet to play the piece in public, merely practiced it in perpetuity for his eventual debut. But five years had elapsed, and the Maestro had concluded that it was time to inform the Protégé of this determination.

'I have made the decision to set a date for our debut.'

The Protégé paled. 'My debut? Am I ready?'

'You will be prepared. I will make sure of it,' he said, with only the vaguest of threat implied. (The Maestro was a demanding taskmaster. He didn't browbeat the boy, per se, but his hand was firmly stern whenever the appropriate occasion arose.) That the boy was one in a thousand, perhaps a million, was not in question. But he was no Mozart, composing by the age of four.

And so the daily rehearsals increased, not only in duration but also in intensity, the Master sometimes bringing his not-inconsiderable nose adjacent with the keys as if he could sniff out any dissonance that his ears had failed to notice.

From first light until well into darkness, he repeated passage after endless passage, leaping through the composition like linear intervals. If anyone were to have looked in on him after he collapsed exhausted into his cot, they would have seen his fingers twitching through the night, as with a dreaming puppy chasing after a ball. But the Pupil was chasing something much more elusive.

The music consumed them both; the Maestro

splitting a reed in order to flagellate the boy if one moment of the thirty-six hours was not as volcanic as he had envisioned.

The Protégé's fingers bled, turning ivory into rubies; the ebony atop his head was streaked with sweat, which soaked his clothing till it was sodden dark with the damp. He shed more weight from his already petit frame, and eyes, once blue, now shared space with a web, shot red with blood. The Maestro maintained this unremitting persistence until the weighty day of the awaited debut.

The recital hall teemed with an expectant throng. There were the classical connoisseurs, the casually curious, and those anticipating the Maestro's inescapable demise. The boy's parents were peacock-proud, though not quite attuned to the son they once knew. His sister, barely aware of her brother, sat and sulked with the enthusiasm of a political prisoner.

For his part, the Maestro remained in the wings, peppering the lad with last-minute instructions. The Protégé was not as nervous as he once might have been, due in part to the mental and physical fatigue which the fervid practicing of the piece engendered. The lights dimmed. The curtain opened. The dissipating murmurs rippled into dust. It was time.

With a pat on his back from the Maestro, (perhaps a gentle assist), the boy walked onto the stage, encircled by an orb of illumination. The audience applauded, (though not as enthusiastically as when he had finished). He pulled out the bench and settled. Opening the first of a multitude of pages, he inhaled, reposed his fingers on the keys, and began.

The first hour was delicately transcendent – dandelion wisps floating in the breeze on a sun-kissed day in Eden, gently belying the eruption still to come. Hours two through six called to mind an alpinist's arduous ascent to a mountainous apex, revealing skill and determination amid escalating danger as he reached each increasing altitude.

Of the dozen hours which followed, entire worlds have been both created and destroyed by the power the Protégé unleashed, an engrossing devourment of paroxysmal proportions, (expelling trouble in every treble and even compelling unrest from the rests). His hands scuttled at the speed of a hummingbird's wings, but with the force and ferocity of a rhino in full assault.

Those who were in attendance recalled the reaction upon the boy's completion: a momentary hush as the final notes expanded into the ether (Christ ascending into heaven), then concussive cheers which could have rivaled Jericho's trumpets; multiple members fainted – not from exhaustion or fatigue or tedium, but from overwhelming rapturous euphoria. A number reported, (surreptitiously, as these subjects were rarely spoken of in polite society), that they had experienced convulsive crescendos – explicit spasms of orgasmic consummation. This eventually ended multiple marriages, the participants appreciating that the sensation would never again be repeated.

The Maestro strode onto the stage and into the maelstrom the boy, (and his own composition), had unleashed. He acknowledged the accolades, the 'bravos' and 'huzzahs' and much accompanying pressing of flesh, not with the relish he had expected, but an ever-increasing sense of dread – a prelude of the realization to come. Something he had not anticipated nor expected.

His only notion, his single focus for all these years, was the priming of his Protégé, not the consequences which would befall as a result of his debut.

A fermata of infinite loneliness resonated within, as he was diminished to a single voice where once there had been harmony. In the beginning, the Protégé had merely been a means to an end. But in the end, the Maestro comprehended everything the boy had meant to him.

Watching as the crowd competed for the boy's favor and being able to touch the pianist to pronounce that they had done so, he understood the boy would never more be his. His Protégé now belonged to them.

DETAILS OF NICK GILBERT
CAN BE FOUND ON PAGE 45

GARDENING LEAVE
Nick Gilbert

"Welcome to 'Gardening Leave', the programme which shows the retired, the redundant, and the basically too bone-idle-to-work how to spend their time usefully – instead of becoming couch-potatoes and watching any old rubbish that's on the telly.

There! I've got your attention already. Even alongside a girl with no bra and not much more brains, I'm infinitely more fascinating.

How do I do it? And as well as Titty, of course, I've got Big Freddie. He's not as photogenic as Titty, and he's certainly not ginger, in any sense of the word, which is good because we need someone a bit butch to do all those jobs that Titty's too feminine for, and I'm too delicate and sensitive to even think about. Like lifting paving slabs, digging out stagnant ponds, and turning on stopcocks that have been turned off too hard.

Tonight we're in Bournemouth at the delightful des.res. of Mr and Mrs Put-Upon, who both love gardening, but find it's got a bit much for them in their golden years. They realised they needed help when, because of his Parkinson's disease, Mr Put-Upon dropped the shears on his leg and slashed an artery and nearly bled to death – because Mrs Put-Upon, due to her Alzheimer's, couldn't remember where the telephone was to dial 999. So we're here to give them a garden makeover. And remember:

you too can try all of these ideas at home.

Dear me, it has got a bit out of control, hasn't it? It resembles darkest Africa in here. Am I allowed to say that? Maybe I should just say tropical jungle.

Anyway, I've sent Freddie to the hire shop to get an industrial brush-cutter, so the dog can see the rabbit. Then we can get stuck in properly. And here he is, back already. Fire her up Freddie.

I say, this really is rather fun: it fairly minces up these overhanging branches. I feel as if I were Leatherface out of the *Texas Chainsaw Massacre*. Christ, that twig nearly got me in the eye.

This cutter gets a bit heavy after a while. Freddie, perhaps you'd better take over and carry on with this, while I talk to camera.

Now that we've finished, we need to get rid of these heaps of brush. As I always say, there's nothing beats a good bonfire. The safest place to have this is slap bang in the middle of the lawn, as anybody who has ever accidentally set fire to a living tree in the middle of a dry summer will tell you. And it can be very costly if they've got Tree Preservation Orders on them too. Not to mention how much the Fire Brigade will want to charge you if they consider you've acted irresponsibly.

I can't help thinking that bonfires have a charmingly rural air about them – although you might find the neighbours start calling you a few rural things too if they're lolling on their loungers over gin and tonics downwind. Don't panic –

they'll soon join in when they see how much fun it is. And for anyone who's concerned about what their bonfire's doing to global warming – think of the petrol you've saved by not going to the tip six times – so you're being very green actually. Just try not to walk through the ashes afterwards, or you'll cover the place with your carbon footprints! Ho-ho-ho. Aren't I a wag?

Whilst on the subject of the environment, no garden is complete without its compost heap at the bottom end; and, remember, the more of your household waste you recycle, the more wildlife you encourage as well. Many are the happy evenings I've spent potting rats with my air pistol with the infrared sighting gizmo. You can use a shotgun, but again it's the sort of thing that suburban neighbours get tetchy about. When you live in the country-proper, as I do, everybody has shotguns so nobody worries about them banging away all the time. Unfortunately, it is far too easy in relatively crowded affluent suburbia to inadvertently shoot someone's beloved dog, or cat, or even child, in the gloaming. That'll certainly put you in bad with them next door – so please do be careful.

The next job we have to do is to clear out those wickedly vicious weeds; I reckon brambles are probably the worst. It's hard to credit that these things are biologically plants, as they've always struck me as feeling akin to green barbed wire. Fortunately, Big Freddie has been to the Army

Surplus shop and come back with a flamethrower, which should sort them out in no time. And if you don't want them coming back, don't, whatever you do, let yourself get fooled into using one of these namby-pamby organic weed-killers. Because they wouldn't hurt a fly. Get yourself some honest-to-God DDT, or sodium chlorate, and let those pesky weeds really know the meaning of scorched earth.

Inevitably, the good work we've been doing will leave shoals of leaves and brush around your paths and patio. So here's a tip from the professionals: don't break your back spending hours pushing a broom: get yourself a leaf-blower with a meaty fifty horsepower of action – one of those that sounds reminiscent of a World War Two air-raid klaxon. Your leaves will be scattered to the furthest recesses of your beds; and, with a bit of luck, most of them will have been powered under the fences into next-door's garden. Try and do it before breakfast. That'll certainly get any lie-a-beds in your street up and ready to make the most of their day; they might grumble at the time but they'll thank you for it later.

Now we've got room to breathe, we can move on to improvements. That pond which had turned into a slime-filled swamp is going to become the central part of our new water feature. Fed via a whitewater ravine through the rockery, from a holding tank containing the Put-Upon's bath water, shaving water, and the outlets from their washing machine and dishwasher, it will be constantly on the move. And they will find it hardly smells either.

In the summer, when all your spare water will be diverted to keeping the lawn alive so that it doesn't resemble a thirty yard square of wholewheat toast, your kids will be so grateful they will play happily for hours in the drought feature that the whitewater ravine has become, among the dog and cat's messes.

It is worth keeping your pond filled though, using a concealed hose, surreptitious midnight buckets if necessary, or even bottled water; because when the neighbours, if any of them are still speaking to you, come round for a barbie and the conversation starts flagging when you start talking about buying a tiger, you can always dig out the trusty old air pistol and pass it round, so they can try their hand at shooting the fish in the pond. The kids will love it. Don't let them use fireworks though: it's considered unsporting in Bournemouth. Remember, your dinner never tastes as good as when you've killed it yourself!

So, there's a bucketful of ideas for you if you want to liven up your own garden when it's getting a little tired. Remember where you heard it first."

THE GUEST
Nick Gilbert

The elephant in the room which was largely a guest in their marriage was the fact that Dan was a werewolf. Ann wished she had known that before she had promised to love, honour, and cherish. Thank God she had jibbed at saying she would obey. Maybe she had a sixth sense, she thought; she certainly must have been lacking something in the other five, because the signs had been there.

The way he sometimes tried to scratch his stomach with his foot was when she later realised that it correlated with the moon being full; Ann knew some people talked in their sleep but Dan howled. The trips to the toilet in the middle of the night which lasted for three hours: to think at the time she had been worried that he might have a bowel problem – if only it had been that simple.

'I should have listened to my mother,' she said to him one night as they lay in bed. 'She was right when she said mixed marriages never work out. What you did on the carpet behind the sofa earlier – I know it wasn't the dog – was too big. And *he* has the sense to do his business outside.'

'Look on the bright side: at least I didn't have diarrhoea. Ann, we've already had this discussion; I was born the way I was; I can't help myself. It could be worse – I could have been bi-sexual.'

'I sometimes think I wouldn't mind you being bi-sexual as long as you were house trained.'

'I try my best but there's no Barbara Woodhouse manual for werewolves.'

'I've never asked what you do when you're out half the night, and I certainly don't intend to start now; but I bet when you're tearing the throat out of some poor woodland creature you know exactly where you are and what you're doing.'

'It's not like that; well, at least not all the time. I enjoy loping through the trees in the dark with my head down. I can see in the dark when I'm a werewolf.'

'Yes, and what are you sniffing after with your head down like a dog, that's what I want to know? I thought I was married to a monster, and I find out you're merely a Jack Russell in werewolf's clothing.'

'It's the thrill of the chase.'

'You're the same as those pathetic twits I see out running in their shorts in the dark at half past six on a winter's morning, when I'm driving to work. Talk about get a life. If I knew that was all I had to look forward to when I got out of bed, I wouldn't get up till the afternoon.'

'I can't help it if I was born to be wild.'

'You'll get caught one night and then you'll lose your job. It's not the sort of thing that's expected of a bank manager. You wouldn't see Captain Mainwaring running round the countryside growling and looking silly, would you!'

'Mmm, I must have missed that episode. Maybe

it's on YouTube.'

'We don't want to go back to living on a council estate, do we?'

'Don't start me off; I remember inner-city living well enough from when I was a kid. Trying to squeeze myself out through a slat window which were-Twiggy wouldn't have got through. I told my parents I couldn't breathe and they would have to put in a casement. My mother wanted to send me to a child psychiatrist and who knows what that would have unearthed?'

'You might have been able to work it through. I mean I understood, eventually, when you told me about it, didn't I.'

'It doesn't work like that. Being a werewolf is a physical thing; it's not the same as having an irrational fear of table lamps or orange paintwork.'

'I suppose so. It was the bed sheets always being covered in hairs that started me thinking. I knew it wasn't the dog. I thought I was going bald at first, but then I realised they were too short to be mine.'

'Anyway you *say* you understood. Only after laughing and taking the piss for months. You didn't really believe me until I stayed in one moonlit night and you sat up and listened to me prowling round the bedroom on all fours with my tongue hanging out and panting as though I'd just beamed in from Transylvania.'

'I thought you'd beamed in from a blue movie until you told me to turn the light on.'

'I can't work the switches when I've got claws, can I?'

'Everybody knows no one's ever going to tell their loved one too many horrible truths at first, so I was waiting for the inevitable weird hobby to come out of the woodwork after we were married – stamp collecting, or trainspotting maybe. But a werewolf. Why couldn't you have had a normal kink, such as rubber, or bondage? Something I could at least have talked about with the other girls at coffee mornings.'

'So that's what you all talk about at coffee mornings, is it? Everybody's husband's perversions.'

'You'd be surprised what some of them get up to. Brian and Josie at Number 10 had to have a new ceiling in their bedroom after the block and tackle brought it down, and the water tank from the attic too. Flooding wasn't covered by their house insurance.'

'Well, excuse me if I don't get too upset by the problems of weekend carpenters.'

'You don't understand, do you? I have to keep telling everyone that you've got no kinks and you're the perfect husband, and naturally they don't believe me. I'm sure they're all laughing at me behind my back.'

'Make something up. Tell them I can only get it on if you dance around the bedroom getting your kit off to the music of "The Stripper".'

'We haven't got "The Stripper".'

'So download it and have a few practices with the lights on and the curtains shut when I'm out for the night. Or tell your girlfriends I'm a Mason, therefore it's top bloody secret anyway.'

'That'll look good in the local paper when I answer the door to a couple of coppers at three o'clock in the morning wearing nothing more than a feather boa. And then they tell me they've dragged you out of a chicken coop at the farm up the road with a hundred shotgun pellets in your backside. And they'd better have been female chickens.'

'I've never heard of a gay werewolf. And I certainly don't want something worse than buckshot in my backside.'

'All right, don't bite my head off. But I do worry about you.'

'I'm very careful. And in the unlikely event I do get caught, I'll make a point of savaging the nearest copper so I get my snout thoroughly truncheoned – then nobody'll recognise me as being from the bank if I get my picture in the paper.'

'We don't want to lose everything we've worked for, do we?'

'Werewolfery is definitely a countryside pastime. I don't want to be ripping out throats in front of an audience of tramps on a bombsite. I hate eating in company – it's a hangover from boarding school trying to enjoy your food in the middle of a load of scrapping feral children.'

'I still have nightmares about council estates; remember, that's where I come from originally.'

'Tell me about it. I remember when we were first married. You can't have a window open at night unless you want to wake up with a knife at your throat, or a gun in your ear. I've woken up halfway through jumping through a closed window before. It was a shattering experience – I had to leave it pulled-to and keep my toenails crossed after that. Then there's making sure you don't land on a car that's freshly torched. There's nutters with machine pistols trying to quietly run their drugs businesses out there and they've got itchy fingers those boys. And that's all if you don't live on the tenth floor – I could have done myself a mischief.'

'You be careful. I do love you, you know.'

'Grrrr. How about a bit of mischief in here. You always say you want me to be a bit of an animal in the bedroom.'

'Yeah; not the sort that craps in the corner though. Come on then.'

'Remember, my love, a werewolf's for life – not just Halloween.'

DETAILS OF ALAN JOSEPH KENNEDY
CAN BE FOUND ON PAGE 164

ECLIPSE THAT
Alan Joseph Kennedy

One more day! Nails shredded, the meagre Persian rug worn bare. Apart from the week-old, mould-covered pizza suppurating on top of the fridge, the flat resembles a nun's cell. This delay is worse than the Stock Exchange rabble before the bell.

Since Eloise Jenkins stopped reading the *Financial Times* and smashed her smart phone and computer with a sledgehammer, the eclipse was uncharted territory till Simon Turner aroused her curiosity.

After trashing an Audi on a test run while buying stocks on the tablet, she resolved not to give into her cravings.

Until his skinny dip in the Mathematical Union's fountain, dressed only in the stolen winner's trophy curtailed his career, Simon Turner was the nerds' pin-up man-child from Silicon Valley to the Kush Mountains.

According to Simon, impatience is a virtue. 'Be in the moment' is his maxim. On the shortlist six times for the Field's Medal, he should know.

When Eloise sips her four morning cappuccinos in Giovanni's café, she seldom flicks through the news, sport or TV pages like regular folk. Electronic devices being taboo, she writes with pencil and notepad, creating the initial scenes of numerous novels. For her, the original burst of ideas turns her on, continuity is a drag and the endings stay unresolved.

Upon arrival, Eloise jots down the first utterance she picks up in the snack bar and starts a story round it for two hours uninterrupted until the character meets Simon. Then she drains the last brown drops of her coffee and chucks the scrunched-up paper in the bin.

Waiting is not Eloise's strongest trait, but Simon's prediction is greater than the collapse of 2009. Not being capable of bringing the date of the event forward is killing her.

Never a skygazer, her neck aches from her latest obsession. The lunar eclipse, a full moon and a blood moon on the same day. A once in a lifetime occurrence. Something Eloise can't control.

Out of her depth, she relies on her genius friend to keep her up to pitch in their regular get-togethers. This week, they've met every two days to thrash out the details.

On the third Thursday of the month, this splinter group of five non-Facebook, non-WhatsApp, non-Twitter geeks have thrown out the internet and congregate in "Leaf Me Alone", the tiniest bookshop in the city, a murky half-lit establishment under the stairs of an unfinished pedestrian walkway.

Simon Turner, the Greek statue lookalike, Maths expert, honours graduate at twelve, worked out the discovery from a 1950's astronomy textbook, a slide rule and a set of trigonometry tables he unearthed in a jumble sale. By hand, he calculated the date of a full lunar, red moon eclipse.

'If you extrapolate the synapse of the elliptical orbit by the satellite axis spins, then deduct from the cube root of the diurnal curvature plus Planck's constant, what you are left with is –, Eloise?'

'It's the – don't tell me.'

'Quite. The denominator to foresee the precise time the earth moves between the moon and the sun.'

'Sounds simp..' responds Monosyllabic Jeff, a Stock Exchange broker recovering from blue screen burn-out. He rarely completes a sentence but always pays for the rounds in the post-meeting pub crawl.

'Simple, once you factor in four hundred times the diameter difference and the ratio of 422 if we measure from the Earth.'

'So, it's – '

'Exactly, Jeff. Two weeping willows, one twenty feet tall; the other sixty feet will seem the same height if the distance is three times greater.'

Simon provokes envy when his perfect mouth pours out these symbols as if they are football scores. Eloise swallows saliva and tries to keep the handwritten notes up to date in the log, but the mathematician's sculpted features, gleaming with passion, captivate her gaze more than his rat-a-tat-tat delivery.

On the evening of the big day, the group meets at eight o'clock. Simon chalks strategies on a blackboard which ends up covered in statistics, cosine figures, integrated equations and incomprehensible squiggles.

None the wiser, Eloise nods like a heavy metal fan on Valium. Jeff and the Boswell twins, Joan and Jim, busy themselves making tuna and chocolate sandwiches. Jim hands out three Red Bulls each.

The chit-chat speeds up till their words overlap more than five Labrador puppies playing together. As the church clock chimes eleven, Simon shepherds his flock into position and mounts the stairs two at a time to the main street, smug in the knowledge that no one else knows their cosmic secret.

The traffic jam reaches the bookshop door before snaking up to Franglin Hill. They aren't alone in knowing about the eclipse. As they cycle past the stream of kids and adults with bent necks, texting, sharing weather reports, Simon eyes the clouds floating away and scoffs. 'Can't they see it's going to be clear?'

Jeff adjusts the timer on his camera. 'What time w...?'

'Not after midnight. Five minutes to.'

It's easier to run through long grass than manoeuvre between the slow marching, hunched figures, so the twins suggest leaving the bikes to stroll up to the vantage point by the monument.

As the quarter to twelve bell fades, they hold their breath. Despite being sardined in by hundreds of bodies, no one around them is watching the cloudless sky. Few appreciate the reddening moon. The eclipse in Sydney over the opera house from eight hours ago absorbs them more. Eloise glances at Simon and gleams. The twins and Jeff link arms. Simon stuffs his hands into his pockets. Eloise wipes her eye with her glove, and peers up.

A myriad of LED lights mars the much-heralded darkness, the silence squashed by the oohs and aahs over the Taj Mahal eclipse. The elegant V of snow geese flying out of the moon's shadow glides above them uncommented. An owl calls for its mate. A silent jet airplane leaves a soft ochre stream. Nobody glances up. Only then ...

The moon disappears at the exact moment of Simon's complex computations, as if sucked through a straw. The reactions of the throng watching it vanish over the pyramids a half hour ago distract them. Above their skulls, a lone goose flies to catch up with its long-gone companions.

Jeff steadies his old Zenith SLR camera, a chunky device from the Soviet Union. He found long exposure film through a friend of his father. 'Grainy, but ... '

The rules of the club forbid YouTube video artists Joan and Jim Boswell from sketching the scene with anything more advanced than charcoal.

The red turns smoky grey.

As quickly as it vanished, the light of the full moon returns. The spectacle is over for another fifty years. The four of them give Simon a well-deserved group hug. He writhes away, like a lizard, from their bodily contact.

'That's that, then. After a good eclipse comes a — '

'Great drinking session.' Four voices in unison.

As they head to the ever-open *Pig and Scratching*, through empty lanes, a cheer and applause from the hill suggest Twitter has uploaded images of the eclipse above their heads. They find a table with no waiting and treat Simon to a pint of scrumpy which he finishes in one.

'Well done.' Eloise half closes her eyes, puckers up and leans over.

'Eh, thanks.' His body swerves the incoming peck as if it were Ebola. Unused to alcohol, he misjudges his seat, trips backwards and smacks the side of his head on the pub floor. Before passing out, Simon Turner slurs, 'Eclipse that!'

Unable to lay her fingers on a mobile in her empty jacket pocket to call a taxi, Eloise pulls out a tube of strawberry lip gloss. She gazes at Simon's tight curls, copper skin, half-opened mouth. Is a tongue allowed in the kiss of life? She bends over and whispers in the mathematician's ear. 'Think of it as a flesh coloured slide rule.'

DETAILS OF SARAH SCOTFORD-SMITH
CAN BE FOUND ON PAGE 54

A MATTER OF CARE
Sarah Scotford-Smith

Maria pushed the tea trolley into Elizabeth's bedroom. A slight breeze wafted in through an open window, flapping the faded velvet curtains back and forth. Elizabeth's bed was below the window; a white feather had gusted in and lay, alone, upon her embroidered eiderdown.

Despite the breeze, the latex gloves Maria wore felt clammy in the warmth of Orchards' Care Home and they kept sticking to the trolley's handle. Trying to get them off was like pulling chewing gum off a desk. Coronavirus made working in a care home an unquestionable challenge.

'Morning, Elizabeth. Do you want a mug of tea?' Maria pushed the trolley across the beige carpet. The mug and a teaspoon rattled against the tea urn as she swerved round a pink rug.

Elizabeth was hunched forward in an upright armchair to the side of the bed. Her pink scalp was visible through thin wisps of white hair. In her hands, she held Margaret Atwood's *The Testaments*. She glanced up; a pair of silver-framed glasses were balanced on her narrow nose. A smile curved her thin lips.

'You look like a spaceman!' she declared.

'It's fetching, don't you think?' Maria reached up and adjusted the visor that covered her face; it was bulky and, because she sweated so much, it persistently slipped down. But at least the home was now equipped with PPE which the government had finally provided. Cara, the manager, at the beginning of the pandemic back in March, had struggled to obtain any.

Letting go of the trolley, Maria walked across the room as if she were on a catwalk. She twirled, showing off her blue plastic apron and matching gloves.

'Ooh, very nice. A bit over the top though.'

'It needs to be. Goodness knows what devastation we'd have if Covid-19 got in here.' Maria walked back to her trolley.

'Poppycock! It's all about control, just like it is in this novel.' Elizabeth held the heavy hardback up in the air. Her spindly arm swayed with the effort. She put the novel back on her lap and bowed over it again. A small lamp on a table provided extra light to help her distinguish the words.

Maria wasn't convinced that Elizabeth understood the seriousness of what was happening. Her world was confined to the care home and the fantasies she uncovered in the books she read. Her only link to the outside – visits from her family – had been suspended. It was hardly surprising that Elizabeth thought she was living in a dystopian world.

Elizabeth glanced up again. 'Got any custard creams on that trolley?'

'Yes, and digestives for Stan and hobnobs for Elsie, Joan and Lily. Everyone's getting their favourites to cheer them up.'

'How is Lily?' Elizabeth arched her neck, which forced the curvature of her shoulders upwards.

'Lonely. She says she feels like a cottage in the middle of nowhere.'

'I'm not surprised. Lily hates her own company. Isolating us in our rooms is all part of the plan.' Elizabeth tapped the novel.

'The only plan I am aware of is the one to keep you safe. If you carry on in this fashion, we'll have to restrict your reading to Mills and Boon.'

'See what I mean? Control.' Elizabeth's eyes widened to emphasise her point, but there was a hint of humour in the crevasses surrounding her mouth.

Maria shook her head. Elizabeth had been a teacher and wanted to keep her mind busy. Too busy at times, Maria mused. She picked up the plate of assorted biscuits and offered it to Elizabeth.

'You're one of the good ones. You haven't been brainwashed. Yet.' This time Elizabeth put her book down on the arm of the chair. She reached out and took a custard cream.

Maria shook her head. 'I need to keep your pecker up until you're allowed visitors again.' She placed the plate back on the trolley and lifted the tea urn. It was cumbersome to hold with sweaty gloves on, and her hand kept slipping down the handle while she poured.

Elizabeth's slight frame collapsed into itself. The

humour around her lips disappeared. 'It's Tuesday today, isn't it?'

Maria nodded.

'My granddaughter used to visit on a Tuesday with her children.' Elizabeth nibbled the custard cream. A few crumbs sprayed outwards and fell onto the skirt of her Paisley patterned dress. 'I haven't seen Eva, her new baby. I love the smell of a newborn; they smell of promise and hope.' She stared at the biscuit aloft in her hand, then popped it into her mouth.

'Promise and hope. That's something we could all do with at the moment.' Maria chewed her lip contemplatively. Not thinking prior to speaking was a bad habit of hers.

All the residents were missing their families. Elizabeth wasn't alone in marking the passing of time by their visits. It worried Maria that the residents would age more quickly without these interactions.

'I know it's hard, but we must keep you and Eva safe.' Maria added milk to Elizabeth's mug from a sturdy white jug.

'God might take me before I have a chance to see her.'

'He wouldn't dare.'

Elizabeth looked towards the window. She was observing the breeze blowing the curtains. She gazed at the feather on the bed. It was rippling in the wind.

'A sign of protection from my Charlie?'

'Maybe. Anyway, you're an obstinate old girl and you're not going anywhere yet.' Maria added a teaspoon of sugar to the mug and stirred it. She had worked at Orchards for three years and knew how the residents liked their tea. If they were forced to spend the final years of their life here, then they deserved special personal touches, such as their carers remembering their particular preferences. That was Maria's philosophy.

Elizabeth twisted back to face Maria. 'Obstinacy and age are no match against God or this Coronavirus, if it exists, and I doubt it does.' She forced a smile, but moisture appeared in her faded blue eyes.

Maria reached for a box of tissues by the lamp. She offered it to Elizabeth. She wanted to hug her, to comfort her. But she couldn't because personal contact with anyone was strictly forbidden. Instead, she had to view a resident's misery behind her barrier of protective clothing.

Elizabeth took out a tissue. She lifted her glasses and dabbed her eyes. 'I can speak to them on the phone, but I can't see my great-grandchild that way.'

'I know, but you will eventually.' Maria put down the box and handed Elizabeth the mug.

'I'm not so sure.'

'Look, I shouldn't really say anything but Cara's trying to organise something for everyone.' Maria had no idea if it would materialise. Cara was exceptionally busy these days, as were all the carers with the additional cleaning they were required to undertake.

'What's she organising?' Elizabeth peered at Maria. Her faded eyes were filled with curiosity.

'I can't tell you anything else because if it doesn't happen, you'll be disappointed.'

Cara's plan involved the full co-operation of all the residents' families, but a percentage of them hadn't responded yet. Cara was adamant that she didn't want anyone to be left out of the event.

'Oh, I already am.' Elizabeth's shoulders slumped. She scrutinised her mug and moved it around as if she was reading the tea leaves.

Maria wished Elizabeth could read the leaves and tell her what the future held. She wanted to know how long Covid-19 would have its hold over the country, let alone the world. The care home had become detached from civilisation. Everything was being delivered, left on the doorstep for the care workers to cart inside.

She and her colleagues were sleeping in a tent in the care home's garden in an attempt at keeping the residents free of infection. Her husband was a paramedic, a frontline keyworker at risk from catching the virus. She missed him and her teenage boys. But, as long as the virus threat level remained high, there was no alternative but to live at the care home. She wondered if she'd have to live in the tent until a successful vaccine was found.

Thinking about her temporary accommodation, Maria stretched. The camp bed made her back ache.

'Oh, I do have some other news,' she said, changing the subject.

'Do you?'

'Yes, Vida's back tomorrow.'

'They didn't keep her in hospital long, did they?' Elizabeth raised her eyebrows.

'No. They needed to free up the beds for more Coronavirus patients. Imagine if she brought it back with her!'

'She won't. It's just a lie, a conspiracy to control us all.'

'Don't start that again.'

'Well, it's true.'

'However much I'd like to argue this out with you, I need to go and change my PPE, wipe the trolley and serve Stan his cup of tea before he sues the home for neglect.' Maria turned around and wheeled her trolley away.

Two days later, to accompany the tea-making equipment, a piece of white paper with a rainbow drawn on it and a pack of colouring pens were placed on Maria's trolley.

'Morning, Elizabeth. I've got an activity for you.'

The window was shut. The sun shone through, glazing the silk eiderdown and making the room stale and airless. The staleness accentuated the bitter odour of urine.

Elizabeth was sitting upright in her chair reading George Orwell's *1984*. When Maria came in, she placed the book on the arm of the chair and peered at the trolley. Her glasses slid down her narrow nose and she pushed them back up with a finger.

'Colouring in! How old am I? Five?' She returned to the novel.

'Don't be like that,' responded Maria as she busied herself with making the tea. A bead of sweat trickled down her forehead beneath her visor. 'Cara thought you'd enjoy colouring in a rainbow in support of the NHS. Lily is planning on opening her window to clap for them tonight.'

'I won't be colouring in a rainbow or clapping.' Elizabeth lifted the novel and obscured her face.

'I'll leave these here in case you change your mind.' Maria gathered up the piece of paper and the colouring pens and placed them on the table by the lamp. Strange how the older generation behave like children, she mused. She poured milk into Elizabeth's tea and stirred in a spoonful of sugar. Lifting the mug, she waited for Elizabeth to put the book down.

'Tea and biscuits?' she asked when Elizabeth didn't lower it.

'Custard creams?'

'Would I forget?'

Elizabeth laid the book down on the arm of the

chair and accepted the extended mug.

'Why were you holding the book so close? Are your eyes troubling you?' Maria picked up the plate of biscuits.

'No, the socket is loose which means I can't use the lamp and, without it, I struggle to see the words.' Elizabeth pointed to where the socket had come adrift from the plaster; there were loose wires hanging out. They were dangerous.

Maria chewed her lip. 'I'll have a word with Cara,' she said, although she was doubtful that Cara could do anything about it. The electrical company who had the contract for maintaining the electrical equipment in the home weren't allowed in to make repairs.

'The Government aren't permitting us to read what we want. They are controlling our thoughts. It's the same in this book.' Elizabeth tapped the novel. She peered at the offered plate and took a custard cream.

'We could move the table and chair around and plug the lamp into a different socket?' Maria scanned the room, ignoring Elizabeth's gloomy ideologies. 'Ah, over there.' Maria pointed to a socket in the far corner by a bookcase.

Elizabeth followed her gaze. 'I prefer sitting near the window.'

'It's merely a suggestion.'

'Can you open it? It's getting hot.'

Maria put the biscuits back on to the trolley.

Some of the residents felt the cold, so she only opened the windows when they asked her to. She leant across the bed and pushed down the window's handle. As it opened, a gust of warm spring air brushed against her face.

'Vida wanted me to open her window as well. She's usually cold but since coming out of hospital she's finding it very hot.' Maria absently chewed her lip. She gazed out of the window at the neatly mown lawn.

A slight breeze ruffled the surrounding herbaceous border and the purple and yellow pansies which stood in a half-barrel in the middle of the lawn. Maria had noticed that Vida had a slight cough. She had informed Cara of that when she had gone back to change her PPE, yet again. Throughout this entire period of Lockdown, Cara had moaned about the lack of available Coronavirus tests. Now, she was attending to Vida, taking her temperature.

Maria stood upright. She glanced at Elizabeth. Her face was tilted towards the window. The gentle wind caressed her skin and lifted her fringe. The wispy strands appeared to be dancing. Her eyes were partially closed as if she were partaking in an illicit pleasure.

'I have some good news,' Maria announced.

'Do you?' Elizabeth twisted round, towards Maria.

'Yes, I can reveal Cara's secret.'

'I bet that one's got plenty of secrets. Her smile never reaches her eyes. She's part of this conspiracy theory. She's the one who pulled my plug socket away from the wall.' Elizabeth wrapped her arms around her thin frame.

'Don't you want to know what she's got planned?' Maria rested her hands on her hips.

Elizabeth peeked sideways at her. 'You might as well tell me.'

'She's arranged for all the residents to talk to their families via the internet.'

Elizabeth snorted and slumped further into her chair. 'What good is that when most of us have never even touched a computer.'

'You don't need to have used one before. All you have to do is sit in front of it and Cara will set up the meeting.'

Elizabeth shifted about in her chair, lifted her hands and examined her twisted arthritic fingers.

'You'll be like the Queen.'

'The Queen?' Elizabeth squinted at Maria through her silver-rimmed glasses.

'Yes – on Christmas day when she delivers her speech.'

'Will I get to see baby Eva?'

'Absolutely.'

Elizabeth's lips curved upwards. The smile dimmed slightly. 'I won't be able to smell her baby smell though.'

'No, that'll have to wait.'

Elizabeth shifted in her seat again.

'I'll send in one of the others to help you to the toilet,' Maria said.

Elizabeth's obstinacy stopped her from asking for help. As Maria turned her trolley around, she contemplated changing her PPE for the fifth time that day.

Five days later, on the Tuesday afternoon, Maria pushed her trolley into Elizabeth's room. Cara was already there, setting up the laptop on a foldaway table. Elizabeth was perched in her armchair in front of the table. The armchair had been moved nearer the other plug socket. The bed remained under the window.

Elizabeth sat upright; her shoulders curved expectantly forward. She was squinting at the blank screen in anticipation. The novel, *Ruth*, by Elizabeth Gaskell, rested on the arm of the chair. That's a nice change from the last two, Maria mused.

'I'm going to be like the Queen,' Elizabeth beamed, looking up. She peered back at the screen, impatient to see her family.

'Yes, you are,' Maria said.

Elizabeth coughed. It was wheezy and dry. She took a large gulp of air and squinted at the closed window. 'It's hot. Can you open it?' She gestured towards it with her hand.

There had been a spring frost that morning and

the day remained nippy. There was no breeze to ruffle the herbaceous borders.

Cara glanced at Maria. Their eyes met. Cara carried on setting up Elizabeth's online meeting with her family.

Maria slowly reached across the bed. She pushed down the latch and thrust the window open. Elizabeth had stuck her coloured-in rainbow on to it. Maria marvelled at how well she had kept within the lines. Some of the residents no longer had that skill.

Maria shuffled backwards and turned around. Elizabeth was staring at her. 'I haven't seen you over the weekend. Have you been off?'

If only, Maria thought. She longed to feel the comfort of her husband's arms around her and to listen to her sons squabbling over who was the strongest, the cleverest, or the best looking.

It had been a difficult weekend for the carers at Orchards. Lily had developed a high temperature and Vida was very poorly; she had most of the symptoms associated with Covid-19. Cara was still awaiting tests. Maria craved the normality she had previously taken for granted.

'All ready!'

Cara had saved Maria from answering any further intrusive questions from Elizabeth which might have led to Vida or Lily's wellbeing.

'Hello, hello.'

Elizabeth waved her hands as four faces and a

baby swaddled in a pink blanket appeared on the laptop's screen.

'Look at me, I'm like the Queen,' Elizabeth giggled. She breathed in and the laugh turned into a hacking cough. She clasped her arms around her slight frame. Gripping her frail body, she gazed at the bundle in her granddaughter's arms; downy fair hair protruded from the top of the blanket.

A white feather fluttered in through the open window. Maria watched as it wavered in the air before coming to rest on the eiderdown.

DETAILS OF ROBERT SCOTT
CAN BE FOUND ON PAGE 65

A WALK, A DECISION
Robert Scott

Joe had two and a half hours to choose between two job offers. The international company in the capital wanted a reply by four o'clock. If not them, it would be the family firm in town. A straight choice, but it wasn't simply about the work. It would also decide where he lived for the next few years or so. Of course, whatever his decision, he could resign and move on later. But at twenty-four, if you are not careful, you can fall in love and settle down wherever you happen to be. It was a fork in the road – two futures, two different lives.

It was impossible to think clearly in the house. He had tried every room, even the garden. His parents were keen to know his plans, as was his little sister, who had been especially quiet and weird all morning.

After lunch, he decided to go for a walk.

'Take a coat – it might rain,' said his mum.

He jogged upstairs and into his room. Kneeling on the bed, he leant on the windowsill for a final weather check. It might be a day for summer showers, possibly a storm. The sky was full of gigantic puffy clouds, blotchy streaks of white trailing off to the horizon and, far to the west, darker dirty-looking clouds. A crazy collage of shapes pasted onto a blue background.

He took a light rain jacket and an umbrella.

His sister's door was open. Sarah was sitting on her bed, knees up, with a book. She didn't seem as if she were deeply into it.

He popped his head in. 'I'll just be an hour or so.'

She nodded.

As he sat on the bed, she turned the book over and rested it, open, on her lap, so the illustrated covers showed upside down. She had read loads during the holidays. Too much. She should be out there, running around – if not climbing trees, something; hanging out, teenager stuff. It was far from exciting in the village, but it was safe, and she had pals.

He waited for her to speak. They had talked about his choices often enough – with tears. There wasn't much left to say, but whatever Sarah came out with right then would be important. She bit her lower lip, staring into his eyes full-on. That was her way of thinking and getting ready to deliver her final word on the subject.

'Do what you want, Joe. You've got to leave home sometime. Why not go for the big job and move away now?' She twisted her face into a lips-together smile that had resignation, hope, sadness, and other things he couldn't decipher in a split second. But her smile contained a great deal of meaning.

On the landing, he kissed the tips of his middle fingers and placed them on Davey's door, as he always did before he went out – and at bedtime.

That ritual would go when he moved out. He would have to replace it with something else.

His mum was waiting at the bottom of the stairs. 'Don't be too long, dear.'

'I won't,' he replied.

'And come back quickly if a storm starts. Run, if you have to.'

He laughed. 'All right. I'll do that.'

He knew she would be watching him from the window until he was out of sight.

His dad was out at the car, checking the oil, which he normally did prior to setting off on holiday. Everyone was behaving strangely.

'A walk's a good idea, lad. Best thing for thinking. It doesn't matter which you choose, does it? We'll always be here.'

'Yeah. I'm going up the hospital and back around – an hour or so, I reckon.'

'Well, watch your time – if you decide on the firm that needs to know before four.'

'Yeah, I will.'

Joe put the jacket over his shoulder and the small umbrella in his back pocket. It was muggy, despite the breeze. The warm wind was like an alien invader; not quite the mistral, but unusual to have both warmth and wind concurrently. He was glad to be in shorts. It was too hot for his jacket and would be too windy for his umbrella. But it was too late to take them back home.

The road out of the village passed the most recent

additions to the estate of 1960s semis. Their gardens, the length of two tennis courts, ran down to a hedge bordering farmland. The final cluster of buildings consisted of the scout hut, the army cadet hall, and changing rooms for the football pitch; it had a sandy car park which was only used on Saturdays.

After the last building, the road turned into a country lane, with thick hedgerows protecting fields of cows, as if they were hiding from the world. Outliers from the dairy herd loomed from behind the thickets, massive pale sandy-coloured shapes. Scary at night for the residents. Everywhere was haunted. The village contained an assortment of characters: the pond's Lady of the Lake, a headless highwayman a mile back, an old soldier at the church. The whole caboodle.

The lane dipped into a hollow with a gravel pit at the side, shaped like a bunker which had been created by a bomb explosion. It climbed round a short steep hill, then levelled out to reveal a long low building behind a row of trees. The sensation was one of coming upon a well-kept solid dacha in the middle of the countryside.

Closer up, an expanse of out-buildings appeared, extending beyond a low walled boundary with railings. He held on to one of its spikes and took a breather after climbing the hill. His head had been empty since leaving the house; empty of thoughts about the jobs, anyway. But other issues were bubbling beneath – connections between the route of his walk and his little brother.

Davey's best pal lived in the last house of the village he had just walked past; the two of them used to race around on the pavements on their bikes when they were children, terrorising the pedestrians.

One autumn evening, in good older brother mode, he had walked Davey up to the scout hut for his first meeting, gently teasing him about his new uniform; saying he looked like Che Guevara with his shoulder-length hair and beret. Davey got irritated because he didn't know who Che Guevara was.

On boring lazy Sundays, they used to kick a ball against the wall of the old changing room huts. And, when Davey was eleven, he ran away, leaving a silly note. Joe found him at the bunker and took him home. Memories of him had passed through his head the whole afternoon. Was this walk saying goodbye? Another goodbye?

He pushed himself away from the railings. The plaque by the front gate caught his eye. Opened in 1908, it had been an isolation hospital for those with "The Vapours". Throughout both world wars, it had been a specialist unit for rehabilitation, recovery, healing; "Complex Healing", the plaque said. Difficult to imagine what that was; but maybe the term could describe what had been going on at home since Davey died, with each family member working out how to deal with it in their own way.

In summers, the hospital used to have fundraising Saturday afternoon fêtes. Stalls would appear out of nowhere, as if a travelling circus had popped up by magic. Joe was too young to spot local improvisations, such as the big plastic dustbin of wood shavings which contained hidden lucky dips. For a few pennies, you could fish around in the bin and pull out a colourful plastic packet of an aeroplane or a tiny kite. The white metal coconut shy stands were probably kept in someone's shed or loft. The cakes had pink and white icing, some with hundreds and thousands on. He had gone there with Davey and Sarah when they were both little. Those were happy, carefree days. Just the three of them.

There was no sign of life from the old hospital grounds. No lights or parked cars. It was closed, or closing. Would it become a ruin? For ghosts to live in, if ghosts need somewhere to live. A more probable scenario was that it would be knocked down to rubble. Another brownfield site on a council spreadsheet.

Joe had reached the end of the road. The paving ran out: it turned into a country lane of dried ruts made by tractor tyres, leading to a row of bushes and a wooden stile almost hidden by branches. He pulled the branches back and pinned them behind the fence to save the next walker the trouble of having to do the same.

Over a cattle grid, the track led down to a field, where a green metal footpath signpost pointed towards the edge of the field. The path hugged the hedge as far as a bungalow driveway. Then it was through a hamlet with no church or shop, only a red letterbox.

All that remained of the five-mile circular walk was a winding country road which led back to the edge of the village. A patchwork of gently rolling hills of arable land stretched to the horizon. Roofs of vehicles on the main road to town appeared over the top of distant hedgerows – the only signs of human life.

For over an hour, Joe had seen no one. He had achieved his desired thinking time; an hour's self-counselling, free of charge. But he still hadn't thought about the jobs or moving away. The memory of Davey had followed him at every point of his walk, even now, three years on.

What came to mind was the image of his little sister, sad, in her room; his mum, worried, waiting for him to come back; and his dad, carrying on.

He stopped at a grey metal gate, put one foot on the lower bar and gripped the top one with both hands. It felt rough and cold. Wooden ones were better. The field was empty, the horizon had turned hazy. As the rain started, he looked up. The sky was grey, full of rain. He hadn't noticed the weather change. He couldn't be bothered with the jacket or umbrella. He started home, accelerating, then jogging, then running. Puddles had formed by the grassy verges and were splashing up onto his legs. Not much further to go. The rain stung his eyes. His hair was wet, his face was wet.

'Stupid, stupid,' he said out loud.

That's it. He had finally decided. He wasn't going any place far away, not yet. He would take the job in town, move out after a while, rent a flat down the road. Sarah would know he was not far away. She could get on with her life with him nearby. He could come for lunch on Sundays. They would stay together. All of them.

DETAILS OF IAN STEWART
CAN BE FOUND ON PAGE 100

A PRE-COVID WRITER'S SOLO MEAL
Ian Stewart

A meal taken alone in a restaurant might be the fount of new ideas, or it could be an unhappy solitary event. If the date has failed to show, then it will be the latter. Or will it? Is it a turning-point?

As an opportunity for reflection, you may decide to consider your desirability as a dinner companion, as a date generally; or maybe you want to move on, release yourself from the sadness that rejection engenders and make practical use of the moment. New ideas may sweep into your consciousness. Hold on to them if they do, and give them rein.

Of course, circumstances might not have been as bleak as I've suggested. You may have no choice but to dine alone, or you might want to do it that way, to have the opportunity of an hour's reflection in a quiet place while enjoying a meal and a glass of wine.

Occasionally I've found myself in this situation, mostly when I've been to a meeting and the evening stretches out before me.

Having found an inviting restaurant, I ask for a table at a window, away from other diners. I want to think about the content and the likely outcome of my meeting. Or simply give over to rumination and reflection on my life as it is unfolding.

Perhaps, since I am now more of a writer and less of an attender of business or academic meetings, I might concentrate on shreds of thought that may become my next project.

In this place I am surrounded by people, each talking louder than their companions, trying to be heard, to get a point across.

My chosen location allows me – and it requires discipline to turn off from my surrounds – to gaze at my reflection in the window's glass, or even take notice of what is happening outside.

My mind focuses on things other than the hubbub of the restaurant. I feel myself rise gently above it all, as if I were setting off in a hot air balloon.

The waiter arrives and interrupts my reverie. I give my food order and select a glass of Shiraz. Soon, he returns with the chosen beverage. I take it in hand, sip, and, once more, look out into the world beyond the window.

I see, passing by, tourists wearing caps with insignias telling where they've been; possibly a suited businessman striding purposefully, his briefcase swinging; a couple of neighbourhood kids chucking a frisbee. The life of the street.

My meal arrives. The restaurant is Thai and the dish, stir fry. I sip my drink again and tuck into the meal.

Concentrating on what I could see through the window has allowed me to focus on what the street can say, about how it can address and uplift my writing.

Have I come across a new plot, some interesting characters? No noise invades my mind. I take out a notebook and pencil.

❀ ❀ ❀

PAPERBACKS PUBLISHED BY
AUDIOARCADIA.COM
AVAILABLE ON AMAZON WEBSITES

A Grave Temptation
A Mature Student in China
A Selection of Short Stories
About St Leonard's
Ain't Life Great!
An Eclectic Mix – Volumes 1-10
Black Secrets
Climbing the Mast
Cyber Pathways
DarkFire at the Edge of Time
DarkFire Continuum
DarkFire Warrior
Ethereal Voices
Mary, A Twentieth Century Life
Nightworld
Odd Angles on the 1950s
On Another Plane
Spatial Zones
The Black Arts
The Deelham Ghost
The Otio in Negotio
Tiernan's Wake
To Insanity and Beyond
Troubling Tales
Where Do I Belong?
Zonal Horizons

AUDIOBOOKS AVAILABLE ON AUDIBLE.CO.UK/AUDIBLE.COM (LISTED UNDER "THE LINDSAY PLAYERS")

A Fireside Tale
A Selection of Fairy Tales from "Tales of Old Japan"
An Actor's Life
An Elemental Horror
Anthony Blair Captain of School
Audio Arcadia's Short Stories – Volumes 1 and 2
The Mind of Mr J G Reeder
Chinese Classic Stories
Clair de Lune and The Necklace
Lady of Secrets and Other Stories
My Life Behind Bars
My Old Home
Tales of the Future
The Carved Pipe
The Enchantress
The Fiddler of the Reels
The Forty-Seven Ronins
The Halfway-House Hotel
The Kent Castles
The Melancholy Hussar of the German Legion
The Poetical Policeman
The Stealer of Marble
The Story of Qiu Ju
The Tailor of Salisbury
The Treasure Hunt

The Troupe
The Visitor, Tobacco and Electronic Warfare
Village Opera
Waiting for Redemption
Wednesdays and Other Stories
Witness for the Defence

ABOUT AUDIOARCADIA.COM

We are unorthodox publishers in that we charge a fee for our comprehensive paperback publishing service — editing, proof-reading (three times), creating cover artwork — and submission of the book to Amazon.

Thereafter, authors receive royalty percentages of net sales of their books from Amazon's websites.

We prefer to think that we offer the opportunity of aspiring writers to showcase their work in the public arena. We are, however, very discerning as to whose work we accept!

We also run on-going short story competitions; full details of how to enter are described on our website at www.audioarcadia.com under the "Competition" tab.

If you wish to receive further information about our company, please email The Editor at rickprod@aol.com

Printed in Great Britain
by Amazon